"Um . . . guys?" Andie was the first one to break the quiet. "How are we supposed to purify water if we don't have iodine, don't have chlorine, and don't have anything to boil it in?"

"I was just wondering the same thing," Pacey said. He pulled off his day-pack and sat on it. "I don't know about you, but I don't want to get some strange North Carolina spotted water disease."

Jen looked all around, her senses on full alert. "I don't know yet. But I do know that we've only got about five daylight hours left. And a helluva lot of work to do before nightfall. If we don't get started, we're going to be miserable later."

No one moved. No one said anything.

"Get started, as in *now,*" Jen added firmly.

Don't miss any of these
DAWSON'S CREEK™ books
featuring your favorite characters!

Dawson's Creek™ The Beginning of Everything Else
A novelization based on the hit television show
produced by Columbia TriStar Television

- New, original stories featuring your favorite characters from **Dawson's Creek™**, the hit television show.

LONG HOT SUMMER
CALM BEFORE THE STORM
SHIFTING INTO OVERDRIVE
MAJOR MELTDOWN
DOUBLE EXPOSURE
TROUBLE IN PARADISE
TOO HOT TO HANDLE
DON'T SCREAM
TOUGH ENOUGH

And don't miss:

- **Dawson's Creek™** The Official Scrapbook
- **Dawson's Creek™** The Official Postcard Book

Available now from Pocket Books.

Check wherever books are available.

Visit Pocket Books on the World Wide Web
http://www.dawsonscreek.com

DAWSON'S CREEK™ soundtrack available on
Columbia/Sony Soundtrax

For orders other than by individual consumers, Pocket Books grants a discount on the purchase of **10 or more** copies of single titles for special markets or premium use. For further details, please write to the Vice President of Special Markets, Pocket Books, 1230 Avenue of the Americas, 9th Floor, New York, NY 10020-1586.

For information on how individual consumers can place orders, please write to Mail Order Department, Simon & Schuster Inc., 100 Front Street, Riverside, NJ 08075.

Dawson's Creek™

Tough Enough

Based on the television series "Dawson's Creek"™
created by **Kevin Williamson**

Written by C. J. Anders

POCKET PULSE
New York London Toronto Sydney Singapore

An *Original* Publication of POCKET BOOKS

POCKET PULSE, published by
POCKET BOOKS, a division of Simon & Schuster Inc.
1230 Avenue of the Americas, New York, NY 10020

ISBN: 0-671-77533-2

First Pocket Pulse printing June 2000

10 9 8 7 6 5 4 3 2 1

Printed in the U.S.A.

For our mini-muse

Tough Enough

Chapter 1

"My one-word review is: yuck," Jen Lindley commented as the final credits of *Deliverance* rolled. She glanced over at Dawson Leery, who sat next to her on his bed. "A gag-inducing display of male testosterone run amok with disastrous consequences for all involved."

"I think you're missing the point," Dawson said. "*Deliverance* is one of the greatest adventure movies of all time."

"As long as you weren't one of the characters who met their untimely demise in it."

"It's not a docudrama," Dawson pointed out. "They're simply actors playing roles."

"In one sense, yes," Jen agreed. "However, it is a given that in watching a film, we put ourselves into the experience; ergo, in a certain way, every film becomes a docudrama."

Dawson gave her a dubious look. "So, what, that means films that dramatize that which we might find personally distasteful are by definition not good films? That's ludicrous."

Jen folded her arms, exasperated. It really irritated her sometimes, the way Dawson was always so sure he knew more than everyone else on the planet about movies.

"Shall we review, Dawson?" she asked. "You had a choice in this movie of being a big-city guy on a wilderness adventure that results in death and mayhem for you and/or your buds, or being a not-so-Beverly hillbilly with somewhat dubious DNA credentials who is out to cause the death and mayhem of you and/or your buds." Jen tossed the VCR remote to Dawson. "Now, rewind to the bluegrass scene, please."

"I thought you hated it. Why do you want to watch it again?"

" 'Hate' is not the point. Besides, I don't hate the movie; I kind of like the movie. And I love the music theme. So please play that part again. It's almost enough to make you like country music."

Dawson sat up against the headboard of his bed and tossed the remote back to Jen. "You do it. I loathe the soundtrack. And I believe the score is bluegrass, not country."

"Whatever." Jen pointed the remote at the VCR and pushed the rewind button. "I'm curious, Dawson. Let's say you thought your life needed livening up. Would you consider taking Jack and Pacey and maybe another guy and go into the wilderness to find yourselves? Our time on Witch Island wasn't enough for you?"

"Possibly," Dawson replied.

Jen snorted back a laugh. "Right, I really see you guys renting canoes on a float trip to nowhere, enjoying a few pints of moonshine with the locals before they set out to decapitate you."

"But you see, that's what's so fascinating about the movie," Dawson explained. "Finally, it comes down to a battle of brains, not brawn."

"Here's the scene." Jen stopped the remote. She pushed the start button and watched, fascinated, as a young Southern boy with approximately three teeth, and a body the result of too much inbreeding, plucked away on his banjo. His fingerpicking turned into a full-fledged bluegrass jam.

"How dextrous," Jen commented. "That kind of talent is almost enough to make you overlook his lack of brains or teeth."

" 'Almost' being the important word in that sentence." Dawson took back the remote and turned off the VCR.

"Meaning?"

Dawson smiled at her. "Meaning you are not, in my experience, a woman to overlook the physical when it comes to attraction."

She smiled back. "Neither, Dawson, are you."

He had to admit, there was some limited truth to that. From the moment she'd moved in next door with her grandmother, escaping the insanity of New

York City, Dawson had been lured by her beauty. On top of that, she was funny, straightforward, and smart.

Which makes we wonder why it is our relationship didn't last, Dawson mused. *Jen decided she needed to figure out who she was before she got involved with a guy again. And then, of course, there was Joey.*

Joey Potter. His best friend forever. The girl who had his heart. Even if they weren't together, which they weren't. It was all just kind of . . . complicated.

Jen stretched out on Dawson's bed like a cat. "You're lucky I live right next door and can come over for movie night," she teased. "Now that Joey's boycotting."

Jen was wrong about Joey boycotting. Sometimes Joey still did come over for movie night. And sometimes they were even able to be together without their history and baggage getting in the way. He didn't know if he should bother telling Jen this or not.

He also didn't know if she'd care.

Actually, I'm not sure these days how she feels about me, Dawson thought. *Or how I feel about her.*

Jen got up and went over to the open window of Dawson's room. It was a warm April night but still early enough in the spring that there weren't any bugs to worry about.

"Mmmm, what a night," she murmured. "Spring on the Upper East Side of Manhattan was never like this."

In his mind's eye, Dawson could see what Jen was seeing. His backyard, illuminated by the lights from downstairs, sloping gently down to the creek. The creek itself—a lagoon, really. It was as much a part of his life as his name. And earlier that evening, it had been filled with hundreds of noisy Canada geese, stopping for a rest and a meal on their migration back north.

The honking had been incessant. But to Dawson, that honking was as beautiful as Jen seemed to find that annoying guitar lick from *Deliverance.* He had heard it every April of his life.

"You can't imagine how different my childhood was from yours," Jen murmured, still looking out the window. "New York City is like a different planet from Capeside."

True. Dawson could picture himself and Joey back in grade school. The two of them would sit on his dock, or Joey's dock, with three boxes of Chips Ahoy cookies, and watch the Canada geese come in for perfect landings on the creek. They'd tell each other everything and watch for hours, or until all the cookies were gone.

More than the thousands of daffodils blooming all over Capeside, that incessant honking on the creek meant spring was here. Really here. Things were being born, animals were mating, couples were falling in—

Stop it, he told himself. *Next thing, you'll be thinking about Joey in her house across the creek. And what she's doing tonight.*

And whether she heard the geese, too.

But it wasn't their time right now. He knew it. Joey seemed to know it, too.

He joined Jen at the window and inhaled deeply. "Nothing else smells like spring."

"A metaphoric and actual time of renewal," Jen said wryly. "Too bad the macho set—Burt Reynolds in that filmic ode to testosterone run amok, for example—only seems to see these things in a sexual light."

Dawson shook his head. "You've lost me."

"Ol' Burt's problem was a basic imbalance of hormones," Jen explained.

Dawson raised his eyebrows, a silent question.

"The movie is basically a series of stupid decisions taken by a bunch of stupid guys, Dawson. Which isn't surprising, considering that when men get together to make decisions, they tend to think with a bodily organ other than the brain. Especially when the sap runs high, so to speak."

"Male bashing is so seventies, Jen," Dawson chided.

She turned to him. "All I'm saying is, if there had been women on the *Deliverance* trip, things would have been different.

Dawson laughed, and a few of the Canada geese still bobbing in the creek startled and splashed in the shallows.

"What's that?" Jen pointed near the dock, where the water was sloshing around noticeably.

Dawson didn't have to look to know. He had seen the same thing just about every spring, in approximately the same place. The snapping turtles were engaging in their mating ritual.

"It's testosterone in action," he said lightly. "Of the turtilic variety. Male snapping turtles getting some action, making little snapping turtles."

"Ah, the circle of life, how touching," Jen said dryly.

"And then they dismember any swimming little fishies that come near them."

"I could weep."

The action in the shallows intensified, and Dawson reddened slightly. It was one thing to have the snapping turtles mate every spring right down below his window, but another thing to have to listen to it while standing next to Jen Lindley.

She wasn't Joey. She could never be Joey. But she was Jen. And sometimes, in some ways, that was even worse.

She flashed him her distinctive, slightly cynical Jen Lindley smile. "Well, Dawson, I have to admit that in some places, testosterone comes in very, very handy."

The night was so quiet—except for the splashing of the turtles in the shallows, and the occasional honk of a Canada goose having a Canada goose nightmare—that Joey Potter heard the slam of the Leerys's screen door across the creek when Jen left.

The screen door had a particular squeak on its springs as it snapped back. *Kah-cree-WHAK!*

No other door sounds like that, Joey thought as she stared out her window. She had lain in bed for hours, eyes wide open, unable to sleep. Then something had made her come over to the window.

Missing Dawson? she wondered. *I wonder if he and Jen just shared movie night. Maybe they watched* Body Heat. *Or* The Postman Always Rings Twice. *Something incendiary that would make both of them—*

"Stop it, Joey," she commanded herself. "You are acting like a major goob, so just get over it."

She glanced at the clock. 11:15 P.M. She knew she should sleep. But she couldn't. She didn't feel at all sleepy.

Maybe a glass of milk would help. She slid her feet into ancient slippers and pulled a sweatshirt on over her T-shirt, then she padded into the kitchen. There, at the kitchen table, sat her older sister Bessie, nursing a glass of milk.

Bessie looked utterly exhausted. It tugged at Joey's heart. It was Bessie, Joey, Bodie, and Bessie's infant son Alexander.

When your mom is dead and your dad's in prison, you kind of end up depending on each other, she thought as she gazed at her sister.

Bessie gave her a weary smile. "Can't sleep?"

"Mind if I belly up to the bar?" Joey asked. "I thought I'd try your home remedy."

"I'll get it for you." Bessie was already on her feet, taking a two-gallon container of milk out of the fridge and pouring Joey a glassful. "Here."

Joey raised the glass. "Here's to getting up tomorrow morning at four o'clock to make breakfast for four idiot fishermen who are the lovely guests of Potter's Bed and Breakfast. Cheers." She took a long swallow.

Bessie sat back down and beckoned Joey to join her. "Their boat pulls out at five; they don't want to be late."

"God forbid," Joey muttered. "Just explain this to me. The posted policy of Potter's B and B is that breakfast is served at eight o'clock. This is not exactly a four-star hotel with room service. And they sure aren't paying us like it's a four-star hotel. So why can't they just get coffee and doughnuts down at the docks?"

" 'A host above all must be kind to her guests,' " Bessie quoted.

Joey smiled sadly. Bessie was quoting from *Thidwick, the Big-Hearted Moose,* a little known Dr. Seuss masterpiece. Their mom had read it to both of them when they were little.

It was a bittersweet memory.

"Do we have to be kind to our guests at four in the morning?" Joey asked, draining her milk.

"We do if we want to pay our bills this month," Bessie replied. "In case you haven't noticed, we're not exactly overbooked."

Joey rinsed her glass at the sink. "You convinced me. When our four suits from Boston in search of a rustic adventure on the high seas off of Capeside come back after a day of fishing and drain the hot-water heater trying to wash their fish guts off, I'll offer to towel them down. When they install themselves in our living room for a cozy evening of Bud-drinking and poker, I'll grab my Hooters T-shirt and offer them—"

"Ha," Bessie barked. "The day Joey Potter puts on a Hooters T-shirt is the day I win the lottery. And I don't buy lottery tickets."

Joey didn't bother to agree. It was implicit.

Bessie rinsed her own glass, then turned to her sister. "If I'm busy with Alexander tomorrow morning, can you help Bodie with the scrambled eggs when you get up?"

Joey thought about breaking eggs into a bowl with milk and mashing them with a fork at four in the morning to feed four basically obnoxious men she didn't know and didn't want to know.

Not fun. However, not being able to afford groceries would be even less fun than that.

"You can count on me." Joey stretched. "I'm gonna go try and get a little sleep. *Very* little, unfortunately."

" 'Night," Bess called.

"You need to sleep, too, Bessie," Joey said, frowning. "I worry about you."

"I'm fine," her sister insisted, even though they both knew it wasn't true.

Joey went back to her room and looked out the window again. Across the creek at Dawson's, she saw the light go out. She could picture him, dropping his jeans on the chair at his desk, pulling his shirt over his head . . .

There was a soft knock on her room. "Joey? Are you asleep yet?" Bessie whispered.

Joey opened the door. "If I was, I wouldn't be now."

"Our guests just informed me they want to get an even earlier start tomorrow."

"Why not just leave now?" Joey quipped sarcastically. "I hear the night fishing is great. Fine, I'm coming, I'll scramble the eggs."

"Breakfast at four," Bessie informed her. "I'll see you in the kitchen at three-thirty."

Joey cringed. "That's cruel and unusual punishment, Bessie. It's probably against the Constitution."

Bessie sighed. "Martial law is in force around this place. Deal with it."

"Sure. G'night."

" 'Night."

Joey climbed back into bed and pulled the quilt up to her neck. She stared at the ceiling and sighed. It wasn't that her life sucked, because it didn't. School was going okay—Principal Green seemed to think there was a good chance Joey would get a college scholarship. And the B and B was getting enough customers to keep the wolf from the door. She had friends. Her artwork was improving.

But there has to be something more, she thought. *What is it I want? Romance? Love?*

Maybe. Or maybe it was something different, something that would test her, push her own limits.

Something that would make her less intimidated by the big, bad world outside of Capeside.

She leaned over and picked up her old-fashioned windup alarm clock. She'd had it for years: it was a green frog's face, and the eyes flipped back and forth with each passing second.

"Rib-bit," she told the clock as she reset it a half hour earlier. "Wake me up at three twenty-five for egg-cracking."

She punched her pillow into shape and nuzzled into it, drifting off to dream.

She was on the top of a snow-covered mountain,

in parka and skis. She pushed off and whooshed down, zigzagging around every obstacle, whipping past the other skiers, completely in control, dizzy with her own power and daring.

The next thing she knew, she was schussing to the base of the ski lodge, where four irate men in funny-looking hats with fishing lures hanging off of them were screaming that she was late and where the hell was their breakfast?

Even in her dreams, Joey came thudding back to reality.

Chapter 2

Pacey Witter plopped down in a seat somewhere in the middle of the Capeside High auditorium and turned to Dawson. "Your father is allegedly a part of this school's faculty. Do you have any earthly idea what this assembly is about?"

Dawson shrugged. "Beats me. Dad didn't say a thing. But then Coach Leery was busy all weekend drawing up next year's football playbook. He's putting in a run-and-gun offense."

"Points on the scoreboard for good ol' Capeside High. What a refreshing concept."

"Believe me, it's still theoretical," Dawson pointed out. "Drawing plays and running plays are two different things."

"Well, I'll sure be rooting for 'em," Pacey said sarcastically. He yawned. "Whatever this assembly is, I'm hoping to sleep through it."

It was Monday morning, and Principal Green had made a special announcement over the intercom during homeroom. Instead of the usual first-period classes, there would be a special assembly program for all juniors. Which was why Dawson and Pacey were sitting in the auditorium, waiting for the rest of their classmates to find their seats.

"Gosh, I love assembly," Jen said, her voice flat. She slid in next to Pacey; Jack McPhee found a seat next to her. A moment later, Joey and Jack's sister Andie sat down directly behind Dawson.

"Ever notice how these things are always about something truly imbecilic?" Jack asked. "Fire Safety Week, or Graffiti Is Bad Week, or some such bull."

"Frankly, I'm thrilled to be here," Joey said. "I was five minutes away from major vivisectional bloodshed in biology."

Jen turned to her. "Just tell them you find dissecting the formerly alive to be morally objectionable."

"I find flunking to be morally objectionable," Joey replied. "It has this dampening affect on the ol' desperate-to-get-a-scholarship record."

"They can't hold it against you," Dawson told her.

"Right," Joey snorted.

"Shhh, you guys, they're starting." Andie took out a clean spiral-bound notebook and opened it to a fresh page, her pen poised over it, as Principal Green ascended the steps to the stage and strode purposefully to the microphone.

"What are you taking notes on?" Joey asked

Andie. "You don't even know what this is about yet."

"I like to be prepared."

"Good morning, Capeside High!" the principal bellowed.

"Good morning," some of the assembled students called back. Most just sat there in their usual Monday morning stultification. But Principal Green was a gung-ho guy. He wasn't about to let that slide. He leaned into the microphone.

"Let's try that again. I said: Good morning, Capeside!"

"Good morning." The response from the packed auditorium went from feeble to tepid.

"Hold it down, please, you're interrupting my nap," Pacey muttered, his eyes closed.

"Ah, yes, that up-and-at-'em Capeside school spirit is alive and well on Monday morning, I can see," Mr. Green said dryly. "You people are young; you should be full of energy! Well, I'm sure when I'm finished talking, you will all have something to cheer about."

"Excellent," Pacey muttered, not bothering to open his eyes. "He's accepted my bribe and is canceling classes for the rest of the school year. If I was awake, I'd weep."

"WAKE UP, PEOPLE!" Principal Green's voice thundered through the auditorium. Even Pacey opened his eyes.

"Much better." The principal smiled benignly at them. "Now that I have your attention. Last month the Capeside Board of Education voted in a new graduation requirement. I'm pleased to announce that your class will be the first class to undertake this exciting addition to the Capeside High curriculum."

"Is foreboding creeping over you, too?" Jen whispered to Jack.

He nodded. "Foreboding and dread, actually."

"I'd like to read the resolution to you at this time," Principal Green continued. He put on his reading glasses and lifted a document. " 'Effective this school cycle, each junior in the Capeside School District must complete a full week's practical education, which shall consist of volunteer field work, special courses, or an alternate assignment selected for them by the school's administration.' "

A low murmur rippled through the auditorium. What did the principal mean? And, more specifically, what did it mean to them?

"In order to give this program—which the board has termed 'SpringPlan'—a fair test," Principal Green continued, "we have decided to implement it immediately, beginning with your class. It means that, instead of your usual spring break, all my Capeside juniors will engage in a SpringPlan activity or course."

The auditorium broke out in a rumble of protest.

"Did I hear what I think I just heard?" Pacey asked.

"Unless we're all living the same nightmare, yes," Dawson replied.

"Doesn't this smack just a little too much of fascism?" Jen wondered. "Since when did Capeside become a police state?"

"Well, excuse me, but I already have tickets to Florida," a cheerleader sitting near them groused. "I am not giving up that to do some stupid SpringPlan."

"How retro. *Where the Boys Are* for the new millennium," Jen said sweetly, craning her head around to the cheerleader.

"Where the who are?" the girl asked.

Jen turned back around, shaking her head at the girl's density.

Up on stage, Principal Green looked down serenely at his students as the noise level rose by the moment. Then he looked at his watch.

"This is crazy," Joey told Pacey and Dawson. "I was planning to work a second job over spring break. Unless Principal Green is planning to pay our mortgage, that is."

"Okay, people, that's enough!" Principal Green banged twice on the microphone, and order was restored in the auditorium. "You've had three minutes to vent your spleens to each other, and that's quite enough. I understand that for some of you, this is going to be a hardship. We'll deal with these on a case-by-case basis. Other than that, I can promise you that there will be no tests, examinations, or papers due for you juniors during the week after SpringPlan, to enable you to catch up on your studies."

"Swell," Jen said sourly.

"And here I thought we'd be studying Chaucer while digging ditches for the homeless," Pacey hissed.

"I'm sure there are a multitude of questions," the principal continued. "I'll take some now."

Andie's hand shot into the air instantly, along with dozens of others.

"Yes, Ms. McPhee?"

"I know the resolution you read said that the administration gets to choose our SpringPlans for us. Don't we have any say in the matter?"

Principal Green nodded. "In many cases, yes. Lights, please?"

In the back of the room, someone shut off the auditorium lights as the school principal clipped on a wireless microphone and went to an illuminated overhead projector. Projected onto a movie screen behind him was a long list.

"Listed here are some—but not all—of the SpringPlan possibilities. As you can see, they range from course work, like a weeklong seminar on 'Multiculturalism and Its Effects on America Today,' to volunteer work with Habitat for Humanity, to distributing food to the hungry, to participating in the 'Reading by Nine' tutoring program in elementary schools."

Principal Green pointed to various items on the list with a laser pointer as he spoke. "And more, of course. The options here are vast, and I'm sure you'll all find things that meet your interests. Your faculty has done a splendid job of preparing this program for you."

"Where's getting wasted with the frat bros on MTV?" a football player joshed, but not loud enough so that the principal could hear him.

"Other questions?" the principal asked.

Emily LaPaz raised her hand. The principal nodded at her.

"If we've worked for one of these charities on our own," she asked, "does that mean we've already fulfilled the requirements for this?"

"No, it doesn't," Principal Green replied. "Although it's a fair question, Emily. And I applaud you if it applies to yourself. But the board has decided that SpringPlan must involve each and every junior. Now, in a few moments, we'll distribute sign-up sheets. You will each get to select your first, second, and third choice. We will make an effort to match people with their choices."

"A seminar on multiculturalism," Jen mused. "Think that means they drop us off in Harlem so we can do field work? There are some great jazz clubs up there."

"Somehow, I doubt that that's it," Jack told her.

"House lights, please?" Mr. Green asked. The house lights came back on. In the back of the auditorium, Tom Brayden raised his hand.

"What about cost, Mr. Green? Who's paying for this, um, learning experience?"

"Good question. In many cases, your labor will help defray the cost of the programs. In other cases, a grant from the state will make up the slack. Anyone else?"

One of the football players stood up. "What if we don't do it?"

"What if you don't graduate?" Principal Green replied easily.

The football player turned red. "With all due respect, sir, that isn't fair."

"Nor is life fair a great deal of the time," the principal said. "If one enforced course of learning or your doing good deeds for ten days is the most unfair thing you ever face in your life, I'd say you're doing very well, indeed. Besides, think how impressive having this on your records will be when you're doing your college applications."

"That's true," Andie said thoughtfully.

For the next ten minutes Mr. Green fielded a few more questions and a few complaints. But after he told the assembled students that the Board of Education was considering extending the SpringPlan program next year to cover both spring and winter vacations, on the theory that students had plenty of time to relax during the summer, most of the complainers shut up.

"Okay, then," Mr. Green announced. "That should do it. Your teachers' aides will now distribute those sign-up forms to all students."

The aides fanned out across the auditorium, distributing sign-up sheets.

"Students, you'll have until the end of today to fill these out. There's a box outside my office to turn them in. If there are no more questions . . . ?" The principal scanned the scowling faces of the assembled students. No one's hand went up.

"Good. You may return to your first-period classes."

"Have you all scanned this SpringPlan list thing?" Pacey asked as he set his lunch tray down to join his friends in the cafeteria a few hours later.

"I hate to be reminded of it over yogurt," Jen said. She spooned some into her mouth.

"Vegetarian Soup Kitchen Cooking?" Pacey asked dubiously, as he looked down the list of SpringPlan possibilities on his sign-up sheet. "You'd think the poor would be hard up for protein, wouldn't you?"

"It's not that I have any objection to doing charitable work or in learning new things," Dawson declared. "But it somehow rankles when it's enforced like this, during what was supposed to be our free time."

"I second that, my friend." Pacey took a bite of his roast beef sandwich, chewed it, and swallowed. "It's enough that we're enslaved here as many hours as we are already enslaved. We now have to offer ourselves on spring break as well?"

Down at the end of the table, Joey had already finished a bowl of soup and was bent over her SpringPlan form, putting light pencil marks next to the things that interested her.

"Well, griping isn't going to change anything, so you might as well give it up," she said to them all. "Whether we like or it not, SpringPlan is a reality. Deal with it."

"What are you choosing, Potter?" Pacey asked.

"I don't think we would choose the same activity, so don't expect to be working with me."

"I am wounded," Pacey replied. "I think we would work well together. You know, me giving orders while you follow them."

"You're delusional." Joey kept her eyes on the list. "I'm thinking I'll either volunteer at the senior center or get trained to lead kids through the Boston Museum of Fine Art. Actually, anything here beats busing tables for ten days."

"Doesn't pay as well, though," Jen pointed out. "Will you be okay?"

"One way or another," Joey murmured.

Pacey crumpled up his sandwich wrapper, spun around, and went for a basket off the rim of the garbage can. "He shoots . . . give him three! Is Play-by-Play Announcing on there? 'Cause I could teach it."

"Sure. Right next to Learning to Invest Your Millions," Dawson told him.

"No, no, my mind is made up." Pacey spun back around to them. "Vegetarian Cooking for the Homeless, here I come. I'll bet there are hundreds of ways to use beans, if only I was exposed to them."

Dawson stared at the list of possible options. Peer Counseling Training. Habitat for Humanity. That was the organization that built houses for the homeless, he recalled.

"Special Olympics would be cool," Jen decided.

"I agree," Dawson said. They shared a smile.

"Well then, it's you and me, Dawson," Jen told him.

Joey cut her eyes at them.

Amazing how Jen can make enforced volunteer work—now there's an oxymoron—sound like a date to have sex, Joey thought.

"How about you, Joey?" Dawson asked. "You up for Special Olympics?"

"I'm thinking more along the lines of Habitat for

Humanity," Joey replied. "After watching our house get transformed into a bed and breakfast, I might know something about pounding nails. And it's a really worthy cause, you have to admit."

"Agreed," Pacey said. "Which is why I'm thinking of changing my middle name to Good Deeds. I think it has a certain ring."

Jen got up with her tray. "I leave you with something my loving, giving, and always optimistic mother used to say. 'No good deed shall go unpunished.' "

"Which means?" Joey asked.

"Call it a premonition, call it negativity, or call it too many years with my dear mother. I don't care what you call it. But you heard it here first—I have a really bad feeling about SpringPlan."

Chapter 3

"Here they are, just what you've all been waiting for."

The substitute homeroom teacher, Mrs. McGill, held up a big manila envelope with the words SPRINGPLAN written on it in bright red capital letters. Dawson couldn't help noticing that the letters were the exact same red as Mrs. McGill's overabundant lipstick.

But maybe noticing something like that was just his way of distracting himself from what was inside that envelope. He'd had many plans for his spring break, all of which involved free time, friends, and his video camera.

None of which involved any of the choices on the SpringPlan form.

He exchanged a dubious eyeroll with Pacey, who

clearly wasn't looking forward to this, either. In fact, no one was. Ever since Principal Green's surprise assembly announcing the implementation of Spring-Plan a few days earlier, the entire junior class had been jittery, argumentative, and just generally ticked off as they waited to hear what their SpringPlan (also known amongst the grumbling students as Spring-Prison) was going to be.

"There's a memo from Principal Green for me to read to you," Mrs. McGill announced, clearing her throat. Her glasses hung by a ruby chain onto what would have been her bosom, if she had one; she lifted them to her eyes and cleared her throat again.

"Oh, that Principal Greenster," Pacey chortled. "What a joker. He's sending us all to Cancún on him. The whole SpringPlan thing was a ruse, right?"

Mrs. McGill shot him a warning look, and Pacey slid further down in his seat.

"Now, then. Principal Green's memo reads as follows: To all juniors—in the envelopes that are about to be distributed are your individual assignments for SpringPlan, along with an information sheet or sheets for that assignment," Mrs. McGill read carefully. "Every effort has been made to match you with one of your preferred selections, though in some cases the school administration has made an alternate choice for very specific reasons. Your SpringPlan assignments are not negotiable. If there is a physical or emotional reason that you cannot safely complete your Spring-Plan assignment, you will need a doctor's note to that effect. We hope you learn everything you can from your participation in this innovative program, and I wish you a wonderful SpringPlan experience."

"Right," a kid in the back of the room snorted. "How soon do we get cuffed to the chain gang?"

Mrs. McGill took a handful of envelopes from the larger manila folder. "Please come up and get your assignment when your name is called, people. Chris Wolfe? Jack McPhee? Dawson Leery?"

One by one, the entire class came up to the front for their envelopes, and a lot of kids tore them open immediately. Some rejoiced at the assignment of their choice; others were complaining and moaning.

Dawson didn't open his immediately. Instead, he laid it on his desk and stared at it as Pacey went to the front of the room when his name was called to pick up his own envelope.

"No time like the present, my friend," he said on his return. "Shall we rip?"

"Let us rip," Dawson agreed.

Together, they opened their envelopes. Dawson's had a single piece of paper in it, with Principal Green's letterhead at the top.

"Dawson Leery," it read. "Please come to my office to discuss your assignment. Mr. Green."

Dawson turned to his friend. "This is very peculiar. For some bizarre reason, mine says to—"

Dawson stopped. Pacey was holding up a sheet of paper that looked exactly like Dawson's. "I'm clueless," Dawson said, shaking his head.

"Ditto," Pacey said.

"Hey," Jack came over to their desks. "Want to see something truly weird?" He held up his SpringPlan assignment. It was a piece of paper that looked exactly like Dawson's and Pacey's.

Dawson stood and scanned his class. "Did any of the rest of you get a note telling you to go to Mr. Green's office?" he asked.

No one had.

"The principal has asked to see you three boys? You may be excused to go see him," Mrs. McGill told them, smiling. Her teeth were wearing half of her red lipstick.

Moments later, the three of them walked down the hallway in silence.

"Why do I feel like we're heading for a firing squad?" Jack asked.

"Maybe—that is, if we beg—they'll at least blindfold us first," Pacey muttered.

They reached the office. Mr. Green's receptionist told them to take a seat—he'd be with them in a minute. Her face gave no clue at all as to why they were there.

"I'm sure he'll want to see all six of you at the same time anyway," she added.

"Six?" Dawson echoed, bewildered.

The door to the office opened, and his question was answered. Jen, Joey, and Andie stepped in.

"What are you guys doing here?" Jen asked.

Jack folded his arms. "I have a feeling the same thing you're doing here."

"In other words, we've all been summoned for the same reason?" Andie asked anxiously. "I hope we didn't do anything wrong. I know I didn't."

"Perish the thought," Pacey muttered.

"Well, doesn't this just liven up the day." Jen plopped down next to Dawson.

"It makes no sense," Joey insisted, leaning against the wall. "We didn't all put down the same choices for SpringPlan. So why are we all here?"

"You get a big 'who the hell knows' on that one, Potter," Pacey replied.

"All righty, one-two-three-four-five-six, I count six heads," the receptionist interrupted cheerfully. "Mr. Green will see you now. He's waiting." She cocked her head toward the door to his office.

The six of them got up and trooped inside. The principal was waiting for them.

"Welcome. Please, have seats." He stayed seated behind his battered desk. "Leery, Witter, Lindley, Potter, and a double dose of McPhee. All present and accounted for. So, I imagine you're curious as to why I summoned you here today."

Andie spoke up immediately. "I would just like to say, sir—and I'm sure I speak for the entire group—we are approaching this new SpringPlan program with the utmost seriousness and—"

Mr. Green cut her off with a wave of his hand. "Take a deep breath, Ms. McPhee. You're not on trial. I have no doubt that you're committed to excellence in every way. I just wanted to explain your particular SpringPlan assignments to you in person, so there would be no misunderstanding."

"That's just the thing, sir," Joey said softly. "We don't have any assignments."

"Ah, but there you are wrong," the principal

grinned. "You do have assignments. I made them myself. I think North Carolina is going to be a wonderful growth opportunity for all six of you."

North Carolina. Huh? Dawson thought. *What SpringPlan is in North Carolina?* He tried to reconstruct in his head the long list of possibilities, but it was impossible. Certainly nothing he'd remotely considered as an option was set there.

"The six of you are an interesting group," Mr. Green continued. "I've been watching you young people for some time. Articulate. Intelligent. Always ready with a quip, a comment, a smart remark. The vocabulary of a college professor and the psychobabble of the thoroughly overanalyzed. Most impressive, indeed."

No one said a word.

The principal sat back and made a tent with his fingers. He seemed to be enjoying himself as Dawson and his friends sat there, stock-still, waiting for the other shoe to drop.

And it did.

"That's why I decided that the six of you deserve my special attention and consideration," the principal continued. "That's also why I decided to exercise my prerogative as chief administrator of this institution and basically supersede your own choices for SpringPlan with one of my own."

"All of us?" Jack asked.

The principal nodded. "Sometimes the man in charge has to do what the man in charge has to do. Which is why the six of you will be spending SpringPlan at Wilderness Camp in North Carolina."

Six jaws fell open.

"Wilderness Camp. You've heard of Outward Bound?" Mr. Green asked. "Well, Wilderness Camp makes Outward Bound look like *Rebecca of Sunnybrook Farm*. Have any of you read that book?"

Andie's hand slowly went into the air.

"I'm impressed, Ms. McPhee. Most young people are unfamiliar with that book these days. It's a classic."

Andie gave him a meek smile. "Uh, actually, sir, I haven't read it. I just wanted to ask you a question."

The principal sighed. "Yes?"

"Uh, physical challenges are not really my long suit, sir," Andie said. "I'm more the cerebral type. And as far as what would be most beneficial on my college application and transcripts—"

"Excuse me for interrupting, Ms. McPhee. You seem to have missed my point. That attitude is exactly why this experience will light up your life," Mr. Green barked. "So, get your sleeping bags aired out. You'll be spending a lot of time in them. That's it. You can go back to class. See you."

Mr. Green stood up and, with a wave of his hand, dismissed them from his office.

They all stood, too.

"With all due respect, sir," Pacey began, even though the principal clearly wanted them out of his office, "I think this is a truly bad idea. I saw a documentary about Wilderness Camp on the news. They make you run naked up a mountain first thing in the morning and then dress you in paramilitary gear and teach you to handle an AK-47. Then you have to go into the woods and kill your own dinner if you want to eat."

"Oh, you could stick to nuts and berries," the principal said. "Be careful with the mushrooms, though, they're not all edible."

"Is this a joke?" Jen asked.

The principal fixed his steely gaze on her. "Do I look like I'm joking, Ms. Lindley?"

"But I've never even gone camping," Andie moaned.

"Mr. Green, I am not a sleep-out-in-the-woods kind of girl," Joey told him. "I still have nightmares from watching the *Blair Witch Project.* Doesn't that prove that this would be psychologically damaging?"

"In a word, no," the principal replied. "And if it would be, I invite you to bring me a doctor's note."

"What I don't understand is why we've been singled out for this," Dawson asked, jamming his hands deeper into his pockets. "We're good students; for the most part we follow the rules, even when they're of dubious merit. And yet it seems as if we're being punished for some real or imagined act that offended you."

Jen folded her arms. "There has to be some way out of this."

"Yes, there is," Mr. Green agreed.

"Well, unless it's multiple choice, why don't you tell us?" Pacey suggested. He was getting testy and didn't much care if their principal-turned-dictator knew it. "Because right now we're contemplating the possibility of early retirement from good old Capeside High."

Mr. Green laughed. "You see, Mr. Witter, remarks like that are exactly why you should be going to North Carolina. You'll learn to canoe, rock climb, pitch a tent, catch fish, which plants to eat and which ones to avoid, and you'll be with high-school kids like yourselves from all over the country."

"Just what does 'like ourselves' mean?" Jen asked.

"Handpicked. Special cases, for various reasons. In the case of the six of you, it is this: At Wilderness Camp, there will be no time to intellectualize. You won't be able to hide behind your facility with language or keep people at arm's length with your witty sardonic repartee. Your very lives will come to depend on qualities of fitness, cooperation, and trust of your fellow man . . . or woman, as the case may be. In short, people, you are about to get down to the nitty-gritty."

"But . . . didn't you say that there might be a way for one or more of us to avoid going to, er, Wilderness Camp?" Joey asked.

"There is," Mr. Green assured her. "What's your least favorite subject, Ms. Potter?"

"Trig," Joey answered without hesitation.

"Well then," the principal said, "if you'd like to forego your stay at Wilderness Camp in favor of seven hours a day of intensive trigonometry study under my direct supervision, just say the word now, and it's a done deal. Same thing goes for any of you. Any takers?"

Silence.

"So you see, I'm not the dictator you imagine me to be," Mr. Green grinned. "You had a choice; you made your choice." He threw his arms wide as if he was embracing them. "Have fun at Wilderness Camp. And if you're exceptionally lucky, I'll be down there to check up on you. Personally."

Chapter 4

Dawson stared past Jen and out the window as the chartered bus rumbled south. Next to him, leaning against the window, his friend was fast asleep.

I wish I were asleep, too, Dawson thought. *That would mean fewer hours of dreading where we're going. Wilderness Camp.*

He shuddered just thinking about it.

The bus had set out from Boston at six that night, with only himself and his friends from Capeside as passengers; a burly, uniformed driver; and a humorless, uni-browed chaperone from Wilderness Camp who'd barked that her name was "Miss Carol."

Two hours later, they had stopped in Hartford to pick up six more lucky students, then in New York City two hours after that to pick up eight more students, and then in Philadelphia a little after midnight to pick up even more students.

And according to Sergeant Carol over there, we're going to be stopping in Washington and Richmond and Roanoke to pick up more passengers before we get to Perreault, which is where this godforsaken camp is located, Dawson thought, as he looked around the already crowded bus.

Where's everyone going to fit all their gear?

Dawson looked behind him. Everyone seemed to be asleep except a guy in the very back of the bus, who was staring out the window just like Dawson had been. He had golden skin and dark hair. Even under his worn leather jacket, his muscles were obvious. When he'd gotten on the bus in Philadelphia, Jen had pronounced him the bus hottie, a cross between a younger Johnny Depp and Ricky Martin.

He seemed entirely self-possessed. And he hadn't said a word to anyone. He was the kind of guy who made Dawson insecure before he even opened his mouth.

It's not like I need to worry about comp for women, though, Dawson reminded himself. *I have a feeling that at Wilderness Camp no one has the time or energy to think about the opposite sex. And if you do, they probably make you swim five miles with a full backpack in your arms.*

He knew he'd better sleep. They were supposed to arrive at Wilderness Camp at one o'clock the next afternoon, and they'd been warned that they would be put directly to work. The first two days at

Wilderness Camp would be devoted to "community service," whatever that meant. It was only on day number three that the Wilderness Camp experience would begin in earnest.

Dread bubbled up in Dawson's stomach like hot larva.

"Hi."

Dawson turned toward the female voice who had spoken to him. It was the girl who was sitting directly across the aisle from him. She smiled wearily.

"Hi," he said back softly, trying not to wake Jen.

She had long, jet black hair braided down her back and a great smile, which she was flashing at him right at that moment. She wore a sweatshirt that read Main Line Volleyball.

Where was she from? Dawson tried to remember when she'd gotten on board. Was it Philadelphia?

"Philly," the girl said, as if anticipating Dawson's question. "I'm Marnie Abrams."

"Dawson Leery, from the great and booming metropolis of Capeside, Massachusetts," Dawson replied, sticking out his hand. "It's on Cape Cod. Hence, Capeside."

Marnie smiled even more broadly. Her grin was infectious. "Clever the way they do that. Tell me, Dawson Leery, how is it that you're going to Wilderness Camp? Somehow, you don't strike me as the guy-in-the-wilderness Wilderness Camp type."

"Wait," Dawson said. "You mean you're doing this voluntarily?"

She laughed. "Is that such a big shocker?"

"Frankly, yes," Dawson said. "I consider this trip one small step from indentured servitude." He motioned with his chin toward Jen. "This is my bud Jen Lindley, and there are four others of us from Capeside."

"So I was right about you. You do have that indoor look," Marnie said. "Like the drama-club guys at my high school. They don't like the jocks. That's okay. We don't like them much, either."

Dawson found himself getting mildly irritated. "Do you always typecast people this way?"

She shrugged. "I just call 'em like I see 'em. Is there any other way?"

"I take it you're a jock."

"Athlete," Marnie corrected. "Three varsity letters—volleyball, tennis, and soccer in the fall. And the last two summers, I've worked as a trainee for the National Park Service in Alaska, which was a total blast. But you didn't answer my question. How is it that you're going to Wilderness Camp?"

"Six of us were basically forced into it," Dawson confessed. "Our principal is sending us."

"Did you do something wrong?"

Dawson shook his head. "You'd have to ask him about that."

"Wow. I guess that would be like someone forcing me to go to musical-theater camp," Marnie mused, then shuddered. "If you're not into this stuff, it's gonna be . . . well, all I can say is, someone must really hate you."

The dread in Dawson's stomach did a backflip. "How do you know so much about Wilderness Camp?"

"My older brother—he's an army ranger—went a couple of years ago. They had to medi-vac him out. Snakebite. It was touch and go for a while, but he lived. He practically jumped out of the helicopter; he didn't want to leave. It was right before his solo."

"Solo?"

Marnie looked closely at Dawson. "You really have no idea what you're getting yourself into, do you?"

Dawson shook his head. "I suppose I don't."

"They put you alone in the woods for forty-eight hours with three matches, your knife, a length of fishing line, and two fishhooks," Marnie explained. "You have to do that in order to graduate."

"So, basically you're telling me that your brother is insane," Dawson clarified, though the idea of a solo in the woods filled him with dread.

She smiled sweetly. "Funny. He'd say the same thing about you. You might want to try and get some shut-eye, Dawson, is it? You're gonna need it."

"Well, so far this is your basic mind-numbing hell," Jen said as they all stumbled off the charter bus for breakfast.

Jack nodded and rubbed his bleary eyes. "I'm already exhausted and we aren't even there yet."

"I've decided to be prepared and have a positive attitude," Andie announced, smoothing out some wrinkles in her shirt. "If we have negative expectations, then of course they'll be fulfilled."

Jack cut his eyes at her. "I love you like a sister, but shut up."

They trouped into the truck-stop restaurant and squeezed into a large booth. All around them, other kids were doing the same, separating by their schools.

"Morning, Dawson," Marnie called cheerfully as she strode by their table like she was speed-walking.

Joey raised her eyebrows at Dawson. "A new friend?"

"More like acquaintance," Dawson said as he opened the coffee-stained menu. "Marnie something, serious jock, from Pennsylvania. Here by choice, if you can fathom such a thing."

"Good mornin', welcome to Tiny's Truckstop, can I get y'all some coffee?" the waitress asked brightly. She wore a pink and white uniform and her nametag read PATSI!

Pacey held out his right arm. "Just shoot it right into the vein, thanks."

"Mainlining caffeine isn't legal in Virginia," the waitress said sweetly as she filled their coffee cups. "And Tiny would have my head if I did it anyway." She motioned to a behemoth of a man who stood by the cash register.

"I can take him," Pacey quipped.

Patsi! smiled. "Be right back to get your orders."

Jen leaned her head onto Jack's shoulder and shut her eyes. "I'm going back to sleep in the hopes that this is all a nightmare and I only *think* I woke up."

"This thing is a relic." Pacey was flipping through the song leaves of the minijukebox on the wall next to their booth. "Look at what's on here. 'Blue Suede Shoes.' 'Be My Baby.' And pretty much every song

Patsy Cline ever recorded. Oh, here's an all-time fave, 'Heaven's Just a Sin Away.' "

"No, no country music," Jen declared, making a cross with her fingers and brandishing it at Pacey. "Not unless it's the theme from *Deliverance*. It's too early."

Too late. Pacey had fished in his pocket for change and already dropped some coins into the jukebox.

"I sincerely hope you're providing a hurl sack if you intend to play that music," Joey said, squinting one eye open.

"What, you and Jen aren't into Patsy Cline?" Pacey asked as he punched some buttons. "I hear she's the official vocalist for Wilderness Camp, even though she died in a plane crash. She had the pipes of Aretha, Celine, and Babs put together. Plus, she could kick your butt. Both your butts, actually."

The opening strains of "Walking After Midnight" filled the diner.

"Who played that?" their waitress asked, hurrying over to them, her pen poised over her order pad.

"I did," Pacey replied.

She flashed him a grin. "You Yankees usually don't have the good taste to play Patsy Cline. That's who I'm named for. My mom loved Patsy so much, she added the exclamation point at the end of my name. And she loved her so much that she didn't want to spell my name exactly the way she spelled hers."

Joey bit her lower lip. "That's really part of your name?"

"If I'm lying, I'm dying," the waitress said. "All righty, y'all ready to order?"

They were. They did. Patsi! hustled their orders into the kitchen.

From behind him, Dawson felt a tap on his shoulder. Marnie was in the next booth, sitting across from an African American girl with dreads who had the tall, sinewy-muscled body of a runner.

"Get some sleep finally?" Marnie asked him.

"Not much."

"The best way to get energized from lack of sleep is to do a few wind sprints," she advised. "Gets the H_2O flowing."

"I'll certainly keep that in mind," Dawson said dryly.

"This is Jana Maleek," Marnie said, introducing her friend. "She's the most kick-butt athlete in our school district. She leaves everyone else in the dust, including the guys."

"She's exaggerating," Jana said, taking a sip of her water. But something in the way she said it made it seem as if Marnie wasn't exaggerating at all.

Dawson introduced his friends.

"So, you were all *forced* to do this?" Marnie asked.

The Capesiders all nodded.

Marnie turned back to her friend. "Sucks, huh?"

Jana nodded. "Whose brain-deficient concept of a good time was that?"

"Our principal's," Pacey replied, leafing through the jukebox songs again. "Just one of the many perks of being the principal's pet."

"Well, enjoy your breakfast," Marnie said. "Go for the high-carb calories. You'll need 'em."

She spun back around to chat with Jana.

"Food, glorious food!" Patsi! sang out, her arms laden with plates. She set Pacey's down last. He had twice as much of everything, plus a doughnut he hadn't ordered. Patsi! winked at him and took off again.

"What luck, Pacey. An option to SpringPrison has just opened for you," Joey said as she put her napkin on her lap. "You can stay here, live happily ever after with Patsi! and Tiny, and have little exclamation-pointed children."

"Sounds like the lesser of two evils to me."

Andie pulled a book out of her mini-backpack and propped it in front of her bowl of oatmeal. Jen squinted at the spine.

"*Survival Training for Dummies,*" she read aloud. "Must we have a reading of this before breakfast?"

Carol, the Wilderness Camp chaperone, marched over to their table. She'd been making the rounds of all the kids' booths. She spotted Andie's book and nodded approvingly.

"Fine choice of reading material," she declared in gravelly tones. "Elementary, but it won't hurt you. You all enjoy your breakfast; it's the last one you'll be eating that you haven't cooked yourself until you're on the bus back to wherever you came from."

"Capeside, Massachusetts," Pacey told her.

"Wherever. Pay attention to the girl who's reading the book. Read!" she ordered Andie.

"Preface," Andie read obediently, spooning some oatmeal into her mouth. "The key word in survival training is 'survive.' This means knowing the laws of nature and not crossing them, because nature will beat you every time."

"Remember that," Carol told them, "because if nature does not beat you every time, I will. See you on the bus in fifteen minutes. Don't be late."

All of them watched her stride away.

"Whoa. Knowing the laws of nature, huh? I plan to pay someone to do it for me," Pacey declared, shaking salt onto his omelette. "Maybe one of the delightful jockettes behind us. I'd rather be poor and stay alive, thanks."

A shrill whistle filled the air and everyone winced.

"W-Cers, you're on the bus in ten," Miss Carol barked. "Eat up and hit the rest rooms."

The regular patrons in the restaurant looked at her with either curiosity, irritation, or amusement, while an elderly couple at the next table stared at Dawson's table, saucer-eyed. The man leaned over and nudged Pacey.

"You kids juvenile delinquents?"

"Yep," Pacey replied solemnly. "Repeat offenders. See that girl?"

He cocked his head toward Andie, who was immersed in her book.

"Yeah, I see her."

"Hot-wired six cars last month, used one of 'em to hold up a Gap store. Got away with dozens of polo shirts. All of them fuchsia. It wasn't pretty."

The woman laughed. "He's pulling your leg, Charlie."

"Maybe," her husband said. "Maybe not." He turned back to his coffee.

"Shovel it in, let's hustle!" Miss Carol bellowed anew.

"I have already developed an intense dislike for that woman," Joey said, draining her orange juice. "Excuse me." She slid out of the booth and headed for the ladies' room. Marnie from Philadelphia overheard her and got up from her both to catch up with her.

"I heard what you just said about Miss Carol," Marnie told Joey.

Joey pushed the ladies' room door open. "I think she's experiencing some gender confusion, and it's making her one unhappy camper. After you."

"Actually," Marnie said, leading Joey inside, "from what I've heard, Miss Carol is a pussycat compared to the rest of the staff. That's why they sent her as our chaperone." She disappeared into one of the stalls.

"Swell," Joey muttered sarcastically as she took in her own tired face in the bathroom mirror. "A pussycat. How peachy."

Jen stretched out her neck muscles and walked down the aisle of the bus. She checked her watch. It was nearly noon, which meant they had to be getting near their destination. As much as she didn't want to be there, she was sick of sitting on the stupid bus, which frankly was starting to smell pretty rank.

Her eyes lit on the great-looking guy in the leather jacket. He had sunglasses on, so she couldn't tell if he was looking back at her.

She gave him her patented Jen smile. "Come here often?"

He didn't move or even say a word.

"Are you sleeping behind those shades, or just hiding?"

"Both," he replied.

"Sleep talking, interesting concept." Jen casually pushed her hair off her face. "So, are you one of the gung-ho set, eager to experience the timeless theme of man versus nature?"

He folded his arms. "Do I look like I am?"

"Are we playing 'answer a question with a question'?"

"I don't know," he replied coolly. "Are we?"

"And would your hostility be aimed at me, this trip, or just life in general?" Jen asked.

"All of the above. Not to be rude, but I'm not into chitchat."

"Oh. Fine. Not to be rude." Jen turned around and went back to her seat. Dawson had moved over to the window, so she slid in next to him.

"Serious case of bad attitude back there," she told Dawson.

Dawson craned his neck around. "Who? Tall, dark, and you-want-to-jump-him?"

"I changed my mind," Jen said. "He's a butt-hole."

"Hey, listen to this, you guys." Andie brandished her book at them from across the aisle. " 'How to start a fire with only a mirror and your brains for company,' " Andie read.

"I really don't want to hear it," Jen interrupted. "I don't plan to be in that situation in this lifetime."

"I don't think they give you curriculum choices at Wilderness Camp," Andie pointed out. "Don't you think we should all be prepared for any eventuality?"

"How about if you prepare and give us the coverage?" Jen suggested. She put her head back and closed her eyes, certain she was heading into the worst week of her life.

Chapter 5

Joey winced in response to yet another blast from the whistle at the end of Miss Carol's lanyard.

"Form a triple line as you get off the bus, let's hustle, hustle, hustle!" Miss Carol boomed. Then she blew her whistle again. "Line up, line up, line up!"

"I'd like to choke that witch with her own lanyard," Joey muttered to Dawson as she scrambled off the bus and fell in line next to him.

"No talking, people; you are not here to socialize!" Miss Carol bellowed. "Don't worry about your gear; you'll come back and get it later. You're all wearing running shoes, as instructed?"

"Bite me," Jen said under her breath.

Miss Carol's head snapped in Jen's direction. "What did you say, young lady?"

"I said 'bright idea,' " Jen ad-libbed, "to have us wear running shoes for our WC experience."

Miss Carol furrowed her uni-brow and stabbed a finger at Jen. "I've got my eye on you, Missy. Now, when I ask a question, what do you all answer? I asked you, you're all wearing running shoes, as I had instructed on the bus?"

"YES!" most of the kids yelled.

Miss Carol's eyes fell on a short, small guy whose skin looked like a science experiment gone bad. He was two rows in front of Dawson, standing next to the great-looking, too-cool guy in the leather jacket Jen had tried to talk with on the bus.

Miss Carol smiled at the little guy. "What's your name?" she asked softly.

"Elliot Windsor," he replied, voice shaking, shoulders so caved in he looked like he was trying to crawl into his own shell.

"Well, Elliot Windsor," Miss Carol said in the same sweet tone, "from your posture, I'd have to deduce that you're a wimp. Would that be correct?"

"Uh . . ." Clearly Elliot had no idea what to say.

"The idea, Elliot," Miss Carol went on cheerfully, "is for you to stand up straight like you have an actual backbone. Anything unclear about those directions?"

Elliot shook his head no.

"And will you be standing upright in the future?"

Elliot shook his head yes.

Miss Carol put her face so close to his that she and Elliot could have massaged each other's tonsils. "You say: YES, MA'AM!"

Elliot cringed. "I'm not hard of hearing. There's no need to—"

"WHAT DO YOU SAY?"

Elliot sighed. "Yes, ma'am."

Next to him, the too-cool guy from the bus eyed Carol like she was a bug under his microscope. Jen studied him out of the corner of her eye. Clearly, he wasn't the least bit intimidated by Miss Carol's drill-sergeant scare tactics.

Pacey leaned toward Dawson. "Is it my imagination, or does Miss Carol have a little hirsute thing going on with her upper lip?"

Dawson bit his own lower lip to keep from laughing.

"I'm serious, Dawson," Pacey insisted. "We're looking at hormones run amok here. Being exposed to this in our formative years could be—"

"WHAT'S YOUR NAME, JUNIOR GUIDE?"

Miss Carol's eyeballs bulged at Pacey.

"Pacey Witter, sir."

There was a snort of suppressed laughter down the line.

"Think you're a wiseacre, huh?" Miss Carol asked. "Drop and give me fifty."

"Fifty *what*?" Pacey asked.

"Push-ups, you weenie," Miss Carol said. "Count 'em off."

"Actually, upper body strength is not something I've cultivated—"

"Sixty!"

"Excuse me, but as I was saying, I'm not—"

"SEVENTY!" Miss Carol got directly in Pacey's face. "Am I understood?"

"Yes, ma'am," Pacey replied.

"Thank you, Mr. Witless. We'll save those push-ups until six tonight, on the quad." She turned to look at the rest of the group. "You see the arch?"

"YES!"

"Excellent. Run toward it. Stay in line. Follow me."

Ms. Carol started jogging in the direction of a wooden arch that had WILDERNESS CAMP carved into the top of it. The group had no choice but to follow.

"I'm getting this *Stripes* flash," Dawson told Pacey as they jogged along. "Where's Bill Murray and Harold Ramis when you need them?"

"Who cares about them," Pacey growled. "The one I want is *Psycho*."

"Stay in line, stay in line!" Ms. Carol shouted as the group ran on. Behind them, they heard the sound of the charter bus roaring away.

"There goes our lifeline to civilization," Jack gasped. "Maybe we can still catch it."

Pacey groaned. "Seventy push-ups. I can't do seventy push-ups in my dreams."

"We appear to be multiplying," Dawson noted as his right foot came down in a mud puddle.

To both the left and right sides of the column of students, approximately a dozen men and women fell in, running alongside. They all could have been models for *Muscle Beach* magazine. They wore plain gray shorts and black T-shirts with the words WILDERNESS CAMP written in plain white dropout-type block letters.

"Prison guards, rejected from Attica for being too tough," Jen deduced. "They look like the Olympic weight-lifting squad. East German when there used to be an East Germany."

"Hey, Dawson, how goes it?" Marnie Abrams swung her head around to ask. She and Jana were in the line directly ahead of Pacey and Dawson, and running easily. Very easily. "Having trouble keeping up?"

"We're doing—" puff, puff, "just fine," Dawson managed.

"No, we aren't," Joey called out from behind him. "We hate it here. We're already planning our break-out. Did anyone bring any teaspoons for digging?"

This first run seemed endless. It took them all over Wilderness Camp, which seemed to be located on the grounds of what looked like a summer camp. They followed a long road that led past playing fields and tennis courts, down to a waterfront where sail-boats and canoes were moored or pulled up on a sandy beach. On both sides of them, all the way down, were green-painted bunks with Indian names painted in red letters on rustic-looking plaques.

"That's where we're sleeping," Pacey said, with more than a little hope in his voice.

"Forget it!" one of the Muscle Beach guys told him. "You'll be dreaming of sleeping there, that's all."

The run continued, and the dirt road veered right, past a large building.

"Let's pick up the pace, junior guides!" Miss Carol bellowed as they started up a steep hill.

"This woman is clearly sadistic," Pacey puffed.

"I'm glad I started my running routine in the morning in anticipation of this," Andie said. She wasn't breathing hard at all.

"Figures," Pacey mumbled.

The hill crested; then they circled past more bunks, playing fields, and cabins. After fifteen minutes that seemed like two hours, the column of fifty kids was brought to a stop in the outfield of a neatly manicured baseball field.

"Are we having fun yet?" Jen panted, her hands resting on her thighs. She sucked for air.

All up and down the column of students, conversations broke out amongst those who were not bent over trying to catch their breath. For once, they were allowed to talk to each other. For a few brief minutes anyway.

Then, a tall, gray-haired man—with the body of a cruiser-weight champion and the powerful jaw and chin of a five-star general—ascended a makeshift wooden platform in front of them, a battery-operated bullhorn in his hands.

"Can you hear me?" he asked, holding the bullhorn to his mouth.

"Yes, sir!" The students had gotten the drill soon enough. Jack rolled his eyes.

"Louder!"

"YE-ES, SIR!"

"Much better. Much, much better." He actually smiled at them. "My name is Clark Santori, and you will be mine for the next seven days. I am the leader of Wilderness Camp. For many of you, the next seven days will be the most difficult days of your life.

In fact, it is my job to insure that they are the most difficult days of your life. It is also my job to insure that they will be the most productive days of your life. You will be thanking me for that later in your life, I promise."

"Gee, thanks, I'm thankful already," Pacey muttered under his breath, but a sharp look from one of the Wilderness Camp instructors shut him up quickly.

"During the next seven days, you will learn what you are made of," Santori went on. "You will face tests, work harder, go further, than you ever imagined you could. You will learn the importance of teamwork. You will learn to trust your life to your partner when necessary. And you will emerge a better man or woman. And now, I will give you one piece of advice to make the next week easier. Think, then do. Think, then do. Am I understood?"

"YES, SIR!"

"Thank you," Santori told them. "Now, get to work!"

"Get to work?" Dawson echoed. "What are we supposed to do?"

He got the answer to his question very, very quickly.

Dawson looked down at the instruction sheet in his hand. Copies had just been distributed to all the campers—called junior guides, or JGs, in Wilderness Camp lingo. And also nametags, which they'd been instructed to wear around their necks on small metal chains at all times: LEERY, Dawson.

Which pretty much means people are going to call you by your last name, Dawson thought. He really wasn't looking forward to being called "Leery." It just wasn't him.

"Just call me POTTER, Joey," Joey said, walking over to him. "This should be right up Pacey's alley. He loves to call me by my last name."

"I have a feeling that the name thing is going to be the least of our worries," Dawson told her as he began to read his instruction sheet.

To: WC junior guides (JGs)
From: Clark Santori, head guide (HG)
Re: First two days' program

Welcome to Wilderness Camp. Your program for the day is as follows:

1. General Assembly on the ballfield
2. Go to Dining Hall by lake for supplies pickup
3. Reassemble on ballfield
4. Lean-to building instruction
5. Police work
6. Dinner (prepared by students from Roanoke, who are excused from police work). This is the only meal that will be prepared as a group until Wednesday. Between now and then, you will be responsible for your own food preparation and cooking. All the supplies you need will be in your pack. You may supplement from the wild. Beware of poisonous mushrooms! (see color photo guide)

7. All campfires must be extinguished by 9 P.M. Reveille and three-mile run tomorrow morning at 5 A.M.
8. Search the list at bottom for name of your WC activities partner. While WC campers will be segregated by sex for sleeping purposes, you will be working with your partner on all other WC activities. You will find a way to get along with your partner. Partner choice will stand. There will be no reassignments.

Dawson scanned the list of names at the bottom of the memo, searching for his own.

"Oh great, I'm dead," Joey moaned as she found the name of her own partner. "I'm supposed to trust my life to Elliot Windsor. He doesn't exactly look like he's built for the WC experience."

Dawson found his name. With a line connecting it to Marnie Abrams.

The jockette and me. Perfect together.

"Hi, Dawson!" Marnie said cheerfully, appearing at his side. "Looks like we're partners."

"I'll just stick with Potter," Joey said. She patted Dawson on the back before going to search out Elliot. "Be careful with him, Marnie. He's fragile."

"Listen, Leery, everyone has to pull their weight on this thing," Marnie warned him. "I mean, I don't mind helping you. But you're gonna have to kick butt. This isn't drama camp."

"What is your problem?" Dawson snapped, clearly irritated. "The machismo thing is already getting a little tired. So give it a rest."

All Marnie did in response was smile. Dawson frowned and looked around them, where people were reading their memos and then looking around for their partners. His eyes lit on Jen. She was talking with the too-cool-to-live black-leather-jacket-wearing guy from the bus.

Apparently Miss Carol had already confiscated his sunglasses.

That left Pacey, Andie, and Jack. Dawson didn't see them anywhere. And the crowd of kids was already starting to drift down to the waterfront.

"Let's go, Leery!" Marnie urged Dawson, tugging him by the arm. "Time to hustle."

"Look, Marnie, unless your life goal is to become the delightful Miss Carol, do you think we could be a little more civil with each other? Treat each other like human beings, little things like that?"

"You got it, Leery," she replied cheerfully and began jogging down the path to the waterfront. "Now, I suggest you haul ass."

Minutes later, they were in the dining room, where senior guides were handing out full backpacks, all of which had nametags on them. Dawson peered into his. Sunblock. Antibiotic cream. Camp clothing in his size, various bags, a knife.

"The suitcases and packs you brought will all be stored until your departure home," the SG in charge announced. "Later this evening you will be permitted to retrieve your hiking boots. Other than that, what is in this pack is going to be your life for the next seven days."

"I'll explain how all that stuff in here works, later,"

Marnie told him. "Unless you consider that to be machismo patronizing."

Dawson reached into his pack and held up a package of freeze-dried something or other.

I'm going to have to eat this? he thought. *How in the world am I supposed to make it? And heat it up?*

"Um, no," Dawson said, thinking that Marnie could turn out to be a key ally in a place like this. "Sorry I snapped at you before."

"I'm the one who's sorry. I assumed you're the indoor wuss type," Marnie said. "Unless, of course, you are."

She lifted her pack onto her back, spun on her heels, and started back to the baseball field. Dawson was close behind her, thinking this was going to be a long, long seven days.

Chapter 6

The sun was low in the afternoon sky on day one at Wilderness Camp, and Jen Lindley was not a happy camper.

Her so-called partner, Chav Martin, had said as little as possible to her all afternoon. He hadn't commented one way or the other on the fact that they were partners. He hadn't given any indication that he found Jen cute, or even remotely interesting.

Mostly, he just did what he had to do and kept his mouth shut.

This place is bad enough, Jen thought. *But do I have to go through the next seven days with the male equivalent of Greta Garbo in her silent-movie phase?*

On their return to the baseball field after getting their gear, Jen and the other JGs had been divided into groups of six, each with a senior guide. The guides had taken them into the woods and given them individual instruction on how to build the lean-tos under which they'd be sleeping, and the fireplaces in which they'd be making their campfire. Then, each pair of JGs would have to build a lean-to and fireplace.

The good news for Jen was that Chav picked up on everything very quickly. The bad news was being stuck with a partner who apparently had no intention of carrying on the simplest of conversations, promising a week of abject torture.

Now all the JGs were back once again in the outfield of the ballfield, ready to get organized for their next assignment: police work. All except the kids from Virginia, of course, who had already gone off to a site deep in the woods where they were preparing dinner.

Jen glanced over at Dawson. It seemed to her that he had lucked out with a partner who loved all this stuff and was great at it, too. Jen had taken notice of the lean-to they had constructed, the one where Dawson and Pacey would be bunking down together.

It's the lean-to version of the Ritz, Jen thought. *Everything except a sound system.*

Marnie had provided their lean-to with pine-bough mattresses covered by pine needles and leaves, on which Pacey and Dawson could rest their sleeping bags. She'd made sure that the thatching on the roof was several layers thick, to keep out any moisture. Jen had even seen Marnie checking the prevailing wind, so that smoke from the fire wouldn't blow directly into the lean-to.

SCREECH! "Police work begins in ten minutes," Miss Carol shouted. "Take a break 'til then."

"Thank God," Jen said, plopping down on her back on the new spring grass. She planned to take advantage of every second of rest offered. She had a feeling there wouldn't be very many.

Her partner Chav just stood there above her, arms folded, his face expressionless.

"Just out of curiosity, Chav, don't you ever chill?" Jen asked, squinting up at him in the late afternoon sun.

He looked down at her. "I chill."

"Pardon me while I check my pacemaker," Jen said up to him. "It's almost too exciting to bear, your stringing two words together and everything."

To Jen's surprise, Chav laughed.

"Oh, so you're human, after all," Jen observed.

Chav sat down on the grass next to her and leaned back on his muscular arms. "Can't escape that."

Jen studied his amazingly chiseled jawline. He really was gorgeous.

"Isn't this the part of the plot where we exchange personal information?" Jen asked. "You know, where we both kind of color the truth to impress each other?"

He looked over at her, sideways. "Why would I do that?"

"Too late, Chav, you already admitted to being human."

He shrugged and looked away from her. "I live in

Philly. Got into some trouble. It was strongly urged that I attend this camp. The end."

"What kind of trouble?" Jen asked.

"You can eliminate major felonies."

"Are we playing twenty questions?" Jen asked.

"One thing you'll learn about me," he began, as he scratched the heart-and-dagger tattoo on his bicep, "is that I never play games."

And that was the end of their conversation. Jen laid there on her back, studying the clouds in the sky, until Miss Carol blew her whistle again.

She and Chav jogged down to the waterfront side by side. But neither of them said a word.

"This really isn't so bad," Andie told Joey, as they stabbed at more garbage with their long sticks, then stuck the garbage into bags that they were carrying. "I mean, picking up garbage at the waterfront isn't exactly what I'd call police work."

"I'm thankful for small favors," Joey muttered, stuffing a used paper plate into her garbage bag. "Not that this is the camp's waterfront. We've already covered a half a mile."

"Garbage sucks," said a tall, blond senior guide, whom Joey had already tagged in her mind as Dudley Do-Right, even though she knew his name was Roger. "Let's get it all. It ruins everything. Only pigs drop it, anyway."

Joey sighed and went after an empty beer can. All around them, the other JGs were doing the same thing. With each full bag of garbage, they'd walk halfway back to camp to deposit it in a Dumpster that was at the edge of the camp grounds. The work was smelly, but not backbreaking.

"Where's Mr. Counterculture?" Joey asked Andie as she stuffed the can into her plastic bag. Andie's assigned partner was a skinny guy from New York with a ponytail and a bad attitude toward authority.

"He got permission to go into the woods to do whatever," Andie replied. "He has a name. Peace. Peace! I asked him if that's his real name, and he says it is now. I would end up with a deadhead as my partner. What year does that kid think this is? I thought he was gonna mutiny when they took away his tie-dyed bandana."

"Does Peace have a last name?" Joey asked. "Maybe Love, or Happiness?"

Andie laughed as Elliot trudged over to them. "How much more of this torture are we in for?" he whined. Sweat dotted his brow, he had the leftovers of someone's discarded fast-food bag on his chest, and he was already sunburned.

"You might want to remember to hit the sunblock, Elliot," Joey said, not unkindly.

"I always burn, no matter what," Elliot said. His face lit up. "Hey, if it gets bad enough, they'll have to send me home, won't they?"

"Elliot," Joey began, "I think you could have typhus and Miss Carol wouldn't even call a slowdown."

"This has to be against child labor laws or something," Elliot said, mopping his brow with the bottom of his T-shirt. "Or against the Constitution. Or something."

"Windsor, would you kindly return to work?" Roger, the SG, asked him. Joey noticed that Roger had not one but two plastic garbage bags full of refuse. Clearly, he was working as hard as any of the students, maybe even harder. "During work time, you work. During yack time, you may yack. Is that clear?"

"Yes, sir," Elliot said, sighing.

"Thank you," the SG told him. "And may you never litter again for the rest of your life."

Elliot ostentatiously stabbed some garbage so the SG would get off his back. "What a steroid case," he muttered.

"No use complaining," Joey told him. She actually thought that because Roger was working, he was entitled to ask Elliot to work, too. "We just have to make the best of it and get through this week."

"I'll be out of here within twenty-four hours," Elliot predicted.

"Look, Elliot, this is not *Revenge of the Nerds,* okay? You're not going to be rescued by a fraternity no one ever heard of. They're serious about this stuff."

"What I lack in brawn, I compensate for in brains," he assured her. "You'll see."

Joey didn't bother to ask what she'd see. Mostly because she didn't want to know.

"Potter quick, hide me!" Pacey hissed, running over to Joey. "We're talking life and death, here."

"Miss Carol propose an amorous liaison?" Joey asked.

"Worse. The partner they assigned me, a female type in the vicinity of normal, just got sent home."

"What happened?" Joey asked. "Did she get in trouble?"

"Nah, her father had a heart attack; I guess that's a valid excuse. And my new partner is—"

"Witter, over here, on the double!"

"Too late," Pacey said. "She found me."

Joey watched as one of the tallest, biggest females she had ever seen strode over to Pacey. Easily six foot three, with the build of a female professional wrestler and the bearing of a linebacker. She actually had a very pretty face, if you had the nerve to look at it.

"Oh, hi, Felicia," Pacey said amiably. "I was just looking for you."

"I weigh in at two-twenty," Felicia said. "I can bench-press you with one hand tied behind my back. It's hard to miss me."

Pacey nodded thoughtfully. "Now that you mention it, Felicia . . ."

"Look, Pacey, I'm not here to make chitchat. We are going to win the Perreault River Award at the end of this week or die trying. Now, let's get back to work."

Joey squinted up at Felicia. "The Perreault River Award. Is that a joke?"

"Of course not," Felicia said. "It's the award for the best team over spring break. My sister and her partner won it last year. But he was kind of a ringer, because his father climbed Mount Everest. This year, it's gonna be me." She turned to Pacey. "Even if I have to drag your lazy butt with me every step of the way."

"Felicia, Felicia," Pacey began, oozing charm, "and I hope you don't mind if I address you by your very lovely first name, it seems to me that—"

"First of all, call me Divine," Felicia interrupted. "Last names keep everything much more businesslike. Second of all, your attempts at wheedling your way into my heart are a waste of your time. Clear?"

"Crystal," Pacey said. "I notice that your stormy eyes turn from blue to black when you're aroused, Felicia. Angry, that is."

Felicia blushed bright red, turned on her size-eleven boot, and marched off.

"Cut her some slack, Pacey," Joey said. "It can't be easy to be that outsized, with a name that sounds like a stripper."

"Felicia Divine," Pacey grunted. "If I come up missing, check our campfire for my remains. I think she plans to hack me to death, then feed me to the flames."

"Witter!" Felicia boomed.

"Coming, lambie-kins!" Pacey called back in a falsetto and dutifully trotted in her direction, his garbage bag bouncing behind him.

"Hike, people. Double line to the dinner site, orderly at all times, people," one of the SGs instructed. "And don't forget your packs. You're going directly from here to your lean-tos to sleep. Okay, move it out."

"Ready, Jack?" his partner said.

"Sure, bring on the fun," Jack replied sourly, and his attitude was as depressed as his voice.

It wasn't that he had a bad partner. She was Darcy Lerner, a girl from Boston, who was both nice and fairly knowledgeable about camping, so he couldn't really complain about that. But it was only the first day, and he was already so annoyed by getting told what to do and when to do it, yelled at instead of spoken to, that his nerves were rubbed raw.

It was all so unnecessary, he thought. *Just some stupid macho game we're all being forced to play. And for what stupid purpose?* He could see, in theory, that it could be challenging to be tested in the woods, even though he had zero interest in the experience. But to be yelled at? It reminded him way too much of his dad. Way too much.

"You okay?" Darcy asked him as they clomped through the woods. Darcy was quite petite—not more than five foot two—and it looked to Jack as if her backpack was as big as she was.

"As okay as I can be and be here," he replied. "I guess."

She flashed a sympathetic smile. "They're probably hardest on us the first couple of days, to break down our resistance. I bet it gets easier."

"You're definitely more of an optimist than I am."

Darcy smiled, and Jack took in her pretty auburn curls and lovely green eyes. *Ironic,* he thought, *that I should get paired with the nice, beautiful girl while Pacey gets a female Attila the Hun.*

"I'm so hungry, I'm actually contemplating eating whatever it is the kids from Virginia cooked," Darcy told them. "In my family I'm known as the picky eater."

Behind her and Jack, Andie walked next to her partner, Peace, who grunted at Darcy's statement.

"All I have to say is, it had better not be meat, because I'm strictly vegan. I think people who kill animals should be tried for murder."

Andie readjusted her pack, which was digging into her shoulders. "So, just out of curiosity, Peace, if it does turn out to be meat, what are you going to do for food?"

"Hunger strike," Peace said, narrowing his eyes.

Andie laughed and then stepped gingerly over a log that had fallen across the trail. "Just exactly how did you end up on this little expedition, anyway?" Andie asked.

"I take full responsibility. I threw red paint on some lady on the school board who was wearing fur. It was symbolic. But the way she freaked, you'd think I had used real blood."

"Well, you must have ruined her coat," Andie explained. "Of course she was upset."

Peace stopped in the middle of the trail, bringing the entire column of students to a halt. He stared Andie in the eye. "How does that compare to her wearing the skins of dead animals?" He looked at her as if she was personally responsible for the concept of death.

Andie just stood there. "Uh . . ." was all she could manage.

"How would you like it if some mink decided that wearing Andie skin would look real cute and keep the mink warm, too?" he asked pointedly.

Andie shook her head and started walking again,

and Peace followed. "I hope you're in serious therapy, Peace," she told him. "That's all I have to say. No. One more thing. I hope that what they have on the menu tonight is nothing but thick, juicy hamburgers."

"How much further is it?" Jen groaned. She was near the rear of the line of JGs, walking with Dawson and Marnie.

"I'd say another quarter mile is all," Marnie replied from behind her.

Jen looked over her shoulder. "How do you know?"

"There was a sign at the trailhead, and it said campsite one, half a mile; campsite two, three quarters of a mile; campsite three, one and a half miles. We passed site two fifteen minutes ago. Site three can't be that far."

"Scary," Jen muttered.

But in just a few minutes, Jen found out that Marnie was absolutely right. They reached the large clearing in the woods where the kids from Virginia had cooked dinner over six or seven open fires. Whatever they'd cooked, the smells wafting from the huge iron soup pots hung over the coals made her mouth water.

"I don't care if it's stewed rattlesnake, I'm eating it," she announced.

"Form a single chow line at each campfire," a tiny female SG named Clarissa called to them. "You'll find your bowls and utensils in your packs. Take as much as you want to eat, but don't waste anything."

"I'm getting this war-zone kinda feeling," Pacey said, edging his way over to Jen, swinging his pack off his back. "Don't shoot until you see the whites of their eyes, or something like that. Do you think I can escape the lovely Felicia for the duration of this dinner?"

"I heard she plans to eat you for dessert," Jen told him.

"That would be funny," Pacey said, "except that I kind of believe you."

Out came their bowls, and one of the Virginia kids ladled some kind of brown, lumpy stew into their bowls, another plopped some reconstituted mashed potatoes on top of the stew, and still another ladled on some lumpy brown gravy.

"Well, 'yuck' just about sums this up," Andie said, staring into her bowl. "On the other hand, it's almost worth it just to see what Peace will do."

Then they looked for someplace to sit.

"No picnic tables," Pacey observed. "A woefully underequipped campsite."

Then Jen got the bright idea of using their packs as chairs, which is just what they did. And the food, which had looked pretty dubious, turned out to be extraordinarily tasty.

"I don't even like food groups to touch," Elliot said, making a face at the concoction in his bowl. He had followed Joey like a lapdog over to where she had joined Jen.

"You'd better eat it," Joey advised him. "We're gonna be burning a lot of calories."

Jen was so hungry, she practically inhaled her bowl of food. "I'm getting more," she said, standing up.

"Go for it," Joey told her. "No need to hold back."

Jen went to the food line. Chav was standing there, having just filled his bowl for the first time.

"How is it?" he asked her.

"Surprisingly good," Jen replied. "Although I am experiencing something of a sugar jones."

Chav reached into his back pocket, took a quick look around to make sure no SGs were watching, and pulled out a Hershey bar.

"Contraband," he told Jen, slipping it to her.

"Are you sure—?"

"There's more where that came from," Chav assured her. "Trust me, I know how to score food."

"Thanks." Jen unwrapped the candy bar carefully and slipped tiny pieces of chocolate into her mouth, so as not to attract the attention of the SGs.

"This is great," she told Chav.

"No prob," he answered, as Jen saw one of the SGs take a close look at him. Chav saw him, too. He languidly took a bite of his stew.

"Chew and swallow like a good boy," Jen teased.

He did, then grinned at her. "I get the feeling this gig wasn't your choice anymore than it was mine."

"I'd say, trust your feeling." She couldn't help noticing yet again the beauty of his golden skin and sinewy muscles. "You lift?" she asked him.

He shook his head no.

"I just thought . . . you're really cut," Jen observed.

"Lean and mean," he told her. "In my neighborhood, that's how you stay alive."

Before she could ask him what he meant, he set off

for the lakeside to scrape out his bowl with sand and then rinse it in the lake.

Half the girls at the campsite's eyes followed him.

Looks great coming and looks great going, Jen thought appreciatively. *Plus, he's got a chocolate stash. All in all, not a bad partner to draw.*

Not bad at all.

Chapter 7

"Listen up." Roger's eyes scanned the group. Dawson, Marnie, Andie, and Peace sat in a semicircle around Roger. They were all in a clearing near the spot where a meandering stream emptied into Lake Perreault. He waited to make sure he had their full attention. Then he took a knife and ripped at a thornbush.

"What's this?" He held a piece of the thornbush over his head. "Andie McPhee?"

"Part of a bush?"

"Not exactly," Roger told her. "This thornbush piece can be the difference between you and a very unpleasant death where your body might not be found for a really, really long time."

Over the past two days, Roger, the SG who looked like Dudley Do-Right, had turned out to be an okay guy. And now that the community-service portion of their Wilderness Camp experience was over, Dawson and Andie felt lucky to be assigned to Roger as their WC instructor for the balance of the week, even if there was no love lost between them and their assigned partners.

Jen and her partner Chav, and Jack and Darcy, had not been so lucky. This morning, they were at the woods medicine area, under the tutelage of the infamous Miss Carol. As for Pacey and the formidable Felicia, and Joey and the not-so-formidable Elliot, they'd been assigned to work with the director of WC himself, Mr. Santori, at deep-woods survival techniques.

The night before, Pacey and Dawson hung out before crawling into their sleeping bags. That was when Pacey had come up with his nickname for Mr. Santori. "The Great Santori," Pacey called him, after *The Great Santini*, the classic Robert Duvall film. "Maybe we can get Duvall to play him. I'm seeing the trailer. Wilderness Camp—The Movie."

"Somehow I seem to have lost my sense of humor of late," Dawson had replied. "I think Marnie Abrams has that affect on me."

"She's actually quite attractive, in a jockette sort of way," Pacey pointed out.

"All instinct, no soul," Dawson had decreed.

His eyes slid over to Marnie now. She was totally focused on every word Roger said.

"Dawson?" Roger asked.

Dawson's head swung around. "Yes?"

"Did you hear what I just said?"

"No. Sir," Dawson added belatedly.

"I asked, how are your fishing skills?"

"I would have to rate them somewhere between a two and nonexistent," Dawson admitted. "On a scale running from one to a thousand."

"Don't you live in Massachusetts? On the coast?"

Dawson nodded. "But the idea of sticking something on the end of a line to catch a fish holds no appeal for me. I would hardly call it sport. And I don't particularly like the way fish tastes, either."

"What if you were caught in the woods, no food, no water, just a length of string in your pocket, your knife, and a few matches?" Roger asked. "And you found yourself near a stream or a lake that could be full of fish? Those fish could be all that stands between you and the untimely demise of you."

"I suppose in your hypothetical situation, that's true," Dawson allowed. "However, since I wouldn't have gone into the woods in the first place, unless I was shooting a movie there, I doubt that your hypothetical situation would ever become an actual one."

"Life can hand you all sorts of experiences you never thought you'd face," Roger said. He swatted idly at a stray mosquito, and Dawson thought how glad he was that the bugs were not really bad. "But it's not really about that. It's about what it means to know, really know, that you're a self-reliant human being."

Marnie shook her head solemnly.

Great, Dawson thought, seeing Marnie shake her head. *Let her catch the fish. I can capture it on video for the Outdoor Channel. Or something.*

Andie raised her hand. "Although nature is not quite my bailiwick either, I'd be interested in learning."

Sometimes that girl is a major-league suck-up.

"Good attitude," Roger told her. He tossed the section of thornbush he was holding to one side. "We'll get to the thornbush later. Let's start simply. Watch me."

Roger edged his way over to an area of the stream where the water pooled into a quiet pond, then continued its flow. "Step quietly when you follow me," he told his group. "Fish can feel the vibrations."

Dawson and the others watched, intrigued, as Roger got down on his hands and knees at a section of the stream where the water was moving very slowly. Then, the instructor reached his hands up under the bank and looked as if he was cautiously feeling for something.

He waited.

And waited. His face was expressionless, all his energy seemingly concentrated onto his fingertips. And then . . . Boom! His hands exploded from the water. And in them was a foot-long greenish-brown fish, which he tossed up onto the bank. It thrashed around wildly.

"Creek chub," Roger announced. "Dinner for one. Not as good as yellow perch or a bass, but when you're really hungry, you won't complain. What you need to do is—Hey! What are you doing?"

Andie's partner, Peace, had edged over to where the chub was flopping around on the bank. He made a quick grab for it, managed to hold onto it with his left hand, and then tossed it back into the water.

The liberated creature laid on the surface of the water for a stunned moment, then flipped its tail and disappeared.

"I'm saving a life," Peace declared. "A fish's life."

"Oh, really," Roger replied. "And why is that?"

"Because taking that fish out of its environment so that you can teach us how to survive in the woods is cruel. How would you like it if I baited a nice, long pole with something you like to eat," Peace said. "Let's say you're starving. And I stuck that pole in your face. How would you like it?"

"I wouldn't," Roger said evenly. "But back to the fish. Don't you think refusing to catch one and then dying of starvation is crueler?"

"Why should that fish die in order that people may live?" Peace pontificated.

"Excuse me, but Woodstock is in that direction," Andie told him, stabbing a finger eastward.

"People made fun of Gandhi, too," Peace said, folding his arms self-righteously.

Andie groaned. Marnie actually smiled, which Dawson found intriguing. *Not exactly the reaction I would have expected,* he thought.

"Peace," Roger said, folding his arms in an eerie imitation of the kid, "let's say you and I make a bargain."

"Depends on what it is," Peace sneered.

"Here's what I propose: For the next two days, you live off the land. You want to eat only plants? Eat only plants. The rest of us will eat whatever else is available to us. Sound fair?"

Peace looked at the instructor closely. "What's the bargain?"

"If you're good at eating just plants, you won't be hungry the day after tomorrow. If you're not, you'll be ready to eat a creek chub. Your call."

"There's a problem. What if I can't identify edible plants?" Peace asked. "How do I know which ones to eat and which ones can kill me?"

"Then I think you're going to be very hungry. Okay, gang," Roger told them all, "time for you guys to try. Peace, go stand under that tree and guess which plants are poisonous and which aren't. By the way, you'll be dining with me over the next forty-eight hours. Our own private campfire. We'll get to know each other. Oh yeah. I eat what I gather, you eat what you gather."

Peace scowled silently.

"Excuse me, Roger?" Andie asked. "I'm assuming that just because I arbitrarily drew Peace here as my partner, I don't have to follow his misguided example?"

"Correct," Roger agreed.

Marnie nudged a shoulder into Dawson. "You ready to try, Dawson?"

"Sure," Dawson said gamely, getting to his feet. "Why not?"

He and Marnie edged over to the bank of the stream, Andie right behind them.

"It's cold!" Andie squealed as she put her hands into the water.

"Shhhh," Marnie whispered. "Concentrate." She dipped her own hand into the stream, just as Roger had. And Dawson did the same.

"Now what?" Andie asked.

Marnie didn't answer. She was completely still, just as Roger had been. Motionless.

Then, *whoosh!* She grabbed onto something and lifted it out of the water . . . a flopping greenish-brown fish, larger than the one the instructor had caught.

"Good going, Marnie!" Roger called from behind them. "Bass!"

"That was awesome!" Marnie cried, her eyes bright with excitement.

Great eyes, Dawson thought. *She looks almost as if she's lit from within.*

Marnie went over to get her fish. "There's a certain disgusting squirm factor to this," Andie said, making a face.

To Dawson's own surprise, he wanted to see if he could catch a fish in his bare hands, too. So, even as behind him Roger was teaching Marnie how to painlessly kill the fish, Dawson put his hands back in the water. He edged them under the bank, and waited. He felt nothing.

Concentrate, he told himself. *Focus like you focus when you're looking through a video lens.*

What was that? Something brushed by his fingers. *Grab it!*

He clamped his hands shut and lifted the smooth, thrashing fish into the air, tossing it over his shoulder the way Marnie had done.

"Excellent!" Roger called. "Way to go, Dawson! You're a born woodsman!"

"Thanks." Dawson was surprised at the exhilarating feeling of accomplishment he had as he went to look at his fish.

"Hey, don't leave me here," Andie called.

"We're be your rooting section," Dawson called back. "Silently, so we don't scare away your next meal."

Andie dipped her hands back into the stream. She definitely did not want to be the only one besides that idiot, Peace, who couldn't catch a fish.

She closed her eyes and concentrated on her fingers, the rushing water, the subtle motion of something going by and—

"Gotcha!" Andie cried as she felt her hands close around a fish. But then she felt it squirm away. "Darn!"

"Good try, McPhee!" Roger applauded. "You'll get it next time. Okay, let's get to cleaning these babies."

Peace was sitting under a tree, ignoring them. Andie and Dawson traded looks.

"You do know how to clean fish, don't you?" Roger asked.

Andie made a face.

Marnie's hand shot into the air. "I do."

"Clean Dawson's fish. The rest of you, pay attention. Peace, close your eyes. I don't want you to get sick on us."

"I don't find that funny," Peace called from his spot under the tree.

Marnie took hold of Dawson's bass. "If you stick the knife into the fish's brain, it's a painless way for the fish to die," Marnie explained as she did it.

Then, in several quick motions, she opened it, gutted it, and scraped off the scales.

Roger held it up. "Perfect, he announced. "You've done this a lot, I can tell."

"My dad taught me and my brothers and sisters

when we were little kids," Marnie explained. "He said it was immoral to catch fish unless you were going to clean them and eat them."

"So I guess homicide runs in your family, then," Peace called out.

Marnie stopped what she was doing and looked at Roger.

"Go ahead," Roger told her. So Marnie marched over to him and squatted down.

"Let me ask you a question, Peace. When you're not wearing name-brand sneakers, what do you wear on your feet?"

Peace shrugged. "Sandals, usually."

"Yeah? Got any leather ones?"

Peace flushed. It was clear he did.

"Cow skin, Peace. You might want to think about things a little more before you decide that you're the moral arbiter of the world."

Go, Marnie, Dawson thought, looking at his partner with new respect.

Roger walked over and got between Marnie and Peace. "I don't want to rag on you, Peace," Roger said. "It's a good thing to be sensitive to all forms of life. There is nothing—I repeat, *nothing*—that I hate more than cruelty to animals, except maybe cruelty to people. If you are going to kill something, be sure you are going to eat it. And say a prayer first."

For once, Peace had no comment.

"Now, watch this, guys," Roger went on. "Here's another technique that could come in handy. Remember that bramble?"

He picked it up and, with a few quick, deft

motions, cut a section of it about an inch long. It still contained a couple of thorns. Then he sliced a neat notch around the stem.

"What's that?" Marnie asked, intrigued.

"You'll see," Roger told them. He reached into his pocket, took out a small spool of monofilament fishing line, and tied the line around the stem notch, making several turns.

"And so, we have an emergency fishing hook," he explained. "Really good for catfish and eels, since they'll probably swallow it. So we bait it with Dawson's fish's innards—we don't let anything go to waste—and into the water it all goes."

"Sorry, but the innards part is kinda gross," Andie proclaimed.

Roger just smiled and tossed the innards-baited makeshift hook into the water.

"More hooks in the water mean more chances at fish," the instructor chided them. "Get to work."

Andie, Dawson, and Marnie all started to make thorn fishhooks of their own. As for Peace, he was standing under his tree, doing what looked to be some kind of karate moves.

"Boy, would I ever love to trade him in for a human model," Andie groused.

"He's not so bad," Marnie said, as she tore a bramble from a bush. "I mean, I don't agree with him. And he's kind of dogmatic. But I respect him more than I respect people who never dare to think about the ethical side of things."

Dawson gave her an appraising look. "You are quite an interesting girl."

"What makes you say that?" Marnie asked as she pulled a spool of monofilament line from her backpack.

Dawson didn't answer. He had to give it some more thought. But the longer he knew her, the less of a stereotype she became.

"Maybe I could trade with Pacey's partner," Andie said brightly.

"The two of you would kill each other in the woods," Dawson told her.

Their hooks done and baited, they went to the pond, tossed their lines into the water, and stood very still.

Dawson shook his head in amusement as he saw himself, Dawson Leery, the guy who made movie night famous, deep in the outback of North Carolina, holding one end of an emergency-supplies fishing line attached to a thorn fishhook he had made himself, baited with the guts of a fish that he had caught with his bare hands.

Then he felt a tug at his line.

"Whoa," he said aloud. "Whoa!"

There was a sharp pull as a big fish took the bait.

"Got one!" Dawson cried happily.

"Let it swallow the bait!" Roger instructed. It was all Dawson could do not to yank in the line immediately, but it turned out that Roger was right. A few seconds later, the line moved away from him in earnest. Dawson could see it ripple against the surface of the lake.

"Now!" Roger told Dawson.

But Dawson didn't need any prompting. Hand

over hand, he started pulling in his fish. And thirty seconds later, he'd reached into the water and pulled up a tasty catfish, taking care not to let his hands touch the spines that Roger warned could cut him.

"Way to go, partner!" Marnie cried, giving him a spontaneous hug.

It was everything Dawson could do not to hug her back.

And in his mind, after he hugged her, he didn't let go.

Chapter 8

The Great Santori bit the head from the grasshopper and chewed happily. "Yum, yum, yum," he chortled. "Now, we're talking flavor. Anyone have a little curry powder?"

"That's disgusting," Elliot grimaced.

"No. Dying of hunger, that's disgusting," The Great Santori told Elliot. "When you're back home in the big city, Elliot, and you see a creepy-crawly, think Raid. But when you're out here, and you've got nothing to eat, I want you to think dinner. Din-ner. Repeat those last two words, all of you."

"Think dinner," they all echoed dutifully, even Pacey and Joey. They were too afraid that the Great Santori might actually ask them to eat a grasshopper—dead or alive—to refuse.

"Roasting makes them taste better," the Great

Santori went on. "That's why I held him over the campfire at the end of a stick for four minutes. Kills parasites, too. Pacey, you up for a go at one?"

"I'm full, but thanks."

"How about a roasted earthworm? Or maybe a delicious broiled slug? Now those are all things that are good eating."

"I'd be happy to take your word for that, sir," Pacey told him.

"So, let me ask you a question, Mr. Witter," the Great Santori said.

"Ask away," Pacey told him. "You're going to, anyway."

"Quite true. So. Here we are, deep in the woods of western North Carolina. There's a crazed maniac out there who's trying to find you, to feed you earthworms or roasted crickets or even worse. You've lost your map and your compass, but you do have the rest of your supplies. What do you do?"

"You know, I believe I already saw that movie," Pacey said. "Highly overrated, though the gimmick was great."

"Do you think that for once you could refrain from babbling about irrelevant things?" Felicia asked him.

"I bow to your largeness," Pacey said. "I mean your largesse."

"Let's get back to the question," the Great Santori asked. "What do you do?"

"Follow the river downstream?" Joey guessed.

"That's a logical possibility," the Great Santori said.

"One that the *Blair Witch* gang neglected to follow," Pacey pointed out. "One of the many reasons I find the movie—"

"Pacey," Joey interrupted, "you sound way too much like Dawson. Can you just focus, please?"

"Okay, here's a theoretical," the Great One began. "Let's say there is no river, and Elliot here is so anxious to get away from fried-earthworm man that he slips instead of slides and breaks an ankle. What then?"

All four of them looked at each other. Even Felicia was stumped.

The Great Santori struck a match.

"Fire," he said. "A really, really useful invention. Fire creates smoke. Smoke rises. Anything that rises can be seen from above. By fire-prevention towers. By airplanes flying. By infrared secret military satellites that seek out heat sources. They're looking for missiles from unfriendlies, but they might see you at the same time. Do you get my drift?"

"They didn't do that in *Blair Witch,* either," Pacey observed. "Another reason that—"

"So if you find yourself stuck in the woods with a bud who has a broken leg, light a fire," Joey interrupted.

"Not one," the Great Santori told them. "Three."

"Why three?" Elliot asked.

"Universal distress signal," the Great Santori confirmed. "Three fires, three whistle blasts, three of anything. What are they teaching you people in school, anyway?"

"To analyze the poetry of Elizabeth Barrett Browning," Joey answered. "And frankly, I'm starting to find this more interesting."

"Listen guys. I'm going to take a walk," the Great Santori told them. "I want you to spend the next half hour gathering food. Living food. Put it in the bowls that are in your backpacks. Person with the most food doesn't have to eat any of it. Okay? Great. Catch you in a few."

The foursome watched the leader of Wilderness Camp walk away into the woods.

Elliot blanched. "We're supposed to look for bugs and creepy-crawlies and put them in our bowls?"

"You heard the man." Felicia was already on her feet, her eyes searching the ground.

"Better get to it, Elliot," Joey told him. "Or else he might make you eat the contents of everyone's bowl. Without curry powder."

Elliot turned green.

"Hel-lo, termite nest!" Pacey called, crouching near a mound of dirt. "I hear that dinner bell a-ringing."

The other three gathered around Pacey.

"I'm the generous sort," Pacey told them magnanimously. "Help yourself to the little buggers. Save me the fat ones, though."

They all scooped termites into their bowls. And then, soon, the four of them were running from spot to spot, locating grubs, earthworms, crickets, whatever they could catch. Joey found herself laughing as they did it.

To her own great surprise, she was actually having fun.

Jen had after-dinner fire-building duty for her and Chav. That afternoon, their instructors had taken all the JGs through various fire-building techniques, including what to do with wet wood.

It was a good thing, too, because during dinner, there had been a brief but violent thunderstorm. It hadn't lasted more than fifteen minutes, but everyone's woodpile had gotten soaked. Which meant if people were going to have fires, they were going to have to come up with dry wood by some other method.

Jen put another log on the stump and took hold of the eight-pound ax that had been provided her. She stood before the stump, her weight evenly balanced, a wet log upright on the stump.

Whack! She swung the ax as she'd been instructed, from directly over her head. The log split neatly in two. She repeated the process. Whack! Now four pieces. Whack! Now eight. Then, she took the sharp blade of the ax and shaved off kindling from one of the pieces, kindling that she would use to start their fire.

She stopped and mopped her brow. Splitting wood was hard work. But she knew Chav was on cleanup duty after dinner, which was equally hard work. All around her, those JGs on fire detail were doing exactly the same thing she was. The sound of axes slamming into wood, and guys and girls grunting with the effort, punctuated the evening.

"Jen! Looking good!" Pacey called to her from where he was doing exactly the same thing fifty yards away. Jen waved back to him.

"Okay, I've got enough," she said out loud as she surveyed the pile she had split over the first half hour. It was nearly three feet high. "And if not, this is going to have to do."

She picked up the wood she had split and carried it over to her lean-to in three quick trips. The light was fading rapidly, and she wanted to get the fire started before it was too dark to see anything. Carefully, she arranged tinder and kindling in the pyramid shape she'd been taught and then built a simple box-fire arrangement around the pyramid.

Dudley, the SG instructor, passed by as she was arranging the wood.

"Looks good," he told her. "What are you waiting for?"

Jen smiled, struck one of her precious matches, and touched it to the tinder. It caught, igniting her kindling.

And five minutes later, she had a beautiful blaze under way.

"You've got it," Dudley observed. "I'm on to help some of your less-blessed colleagues."

"Thanks," Jen told him. She added another couple of pieces of wood and watched them burst into flame and crackle. She was exhausted from the wood-splitting, and a cool breeze that had come up chilled her body through her clothes. But for some bizarre reason, she felt exhausted in a good way.

She reached her hands out over the flames.

"Don't set yourself on fire," said a male voice, stepping up to the fire from out of the murky twilight. "I'd lose my fire builder."

Chav. Back from cleanup detail. She looked at him. "Aren't you cold?"

"Doesn't bother me."

Jen sat down on a flat rock next to the fire and studied Chav's face. He sat down, too.

"So, what does bother you, then?" she asked.

Chav scratched his chin. "Not much."

Jen shook her head. "You cultivate this strong, silent thing, don't you? You may have watched one too many Clint Eastwood movies in your youth."

"Nope."

"Charles Bronson more your speed?"

"When I was a kid, we didn't have a TV. And we couldn't afford the movies." Chav stared into the fire as he talked.

Jen was silent for a moment. The only person she'd ever known who didn't have a TV was Emberly Cummins, but that was because Emberly's parents considered television to be a sign of cultural inferiority. The Cummins's only watched movies—in their private screening room on the guest floor of their townhouse.

"Did you grow up in Philly?" Jen finally asked.

"We moved there when I was ten." Chav rested his hands on his knees. "Before that, Marfa, Texas."

Marfa, Texas . . . where have I heard of that before? Jen mused. And then it came to her.

"Giant!" she exclaimed. "James Dean—awesome movie. It was filmed in Marfa, right?"

Chav nodded. "And that's Marfa's only claim to fame, believe me. It's a nasty-ass place. I couldn't wait to get out of there." His dark eyes danced in the firelight.

"So, your family just up and moved one day?" Jen asked. "Did someone have a burning desire to live near the Liberty Bell?"

Chav chuckled sardonically. "Not exactly. It was after my brother got arrested for murder."

Jen didn't miss a beat. "Did he do it?"

Chav threw a twig into the fire. "What difference does it make? The Man said he did it. And in the People's Republic of Texas, what the Man says, goes."

"You can't be that cynical—"

"Jen, sorry," Chav interrupted savagely, "but you don't know squat, okay?"

Jen raised her knees to her chin and wrapped her arms around them. "Look, it's fair to call me a rich, spoiled brat. Past tense. I grew up in New York with a lot of overprivileged, morally bankrupt kids. And I suppose that at one time, I was one of them. But you don't have to be poor in order to see the ugly side of humanity."

He shot her an incredulous look and laughed in a way that wasn't funny. "Yeah? So, Jen, if someone set you up for a crime you didn't commit, you think you'd get stuck with some public defender and get lost in a system that sees you as another wetback migrant worker?"

"No, Chav, it isn't—"

"Or do you think maybe Mommy and Daddy would spring for the best lawyers money can buy?"

"Were your parents migrant workers?" Jen asked, her voice low.

"I was named after Caesar Chavez," he told her.

"My parents think he is the greatest man who ever lived. He tried to change the way things are for migrant workers. But today, the same crap goes on. Nothing has changed."

"I'm sorry," Jen said, even though she knew how inadequate that sounded.

Chav stared into the fire for a moment. "My parents begged, borrowed, stole, whatever they had to do, to get us out of Texas. We had cousins in Philly, so that's where we went." He gave her a sardonic smile. "What's funny is, skinheads in Philly look down on the Latino kids just as much as they did in Marfa. Same crap, new town."

"I'm sorry," Jen said again.

"You already said that," Chav snapped. "I'm sorry, too. The whole damn world is sorry. But we still have to live by the rich, white man's justice, don't we?"

Jen exhaled slowly. "Just one question. How do you even stand upright with that huge chip on your shoulder?"

The look in his eyes when he turned on her made her shiver, but she forced herself not to back down. "Look, admittedly, my life experience is nothing at all like yours," she went on. "Believe it or not, you can have white skin and be a good person. You can have money and still experience pain, fear, disillusionment—"

"How about if you save the we-are-the-world lecture?" Chav interrupted. "I've heard it from every do-gooder who's ever gotten in my face. Going on about how smart I am and how much potential I have and I could be such a credit to 'my people'."

He sprang gracefully to his feet. "I don't have 'people,' okay? I've only got myself."

"Chav—" Jen began.

But she was saying it to his back.

He was already striding away.

"He's graceful, isn't he?" Marnie commented to Dawson as she watched Chav stride away from one of the campsites. They were sitting in front of Pacey and Dawson's lean-to, enjoying the warmth of the fire Dawson had built.

"Was that question from a female appraisal point of view?" Dawson asked.

"Of course." Marnie grinned at him. "Or did you think us girl jocks didn't notice stuff like that?"

"Now that you mention it—"

Marnie playfully nudged his shoulder. "Gotta watch those stereotypes, Leery. They can be dangerous."

"Point well taken."

Marnie cocked her head at him. "You did really well today, you know."

He was ridiculously pleased by her compliment, so pleased that he surprised himself. A memory of flipping the catfish he'd caught using the thorn hook up onto the bank flashed into his head. That was cool.

"You think so?" he asked.

"For a guy who considers experiencing the great outdoors watching *Out of Africa*, yes," Marnie teased.

"It's just that all this seems so unnecessary," Dawson explained. "What was the twentieth century about, if not man's triumph over nature? Why should we play these silly games where we romanticize doing things that humankind has worked so hard not to have to do anymore?"

She leaned back contemplatively on her elbows. "I guess . . . to test ourselves. To face our own fears. To go past them."

Dawson shrugged. "But why?"

"Because it translates to every other facet of your life, Dawson."

"Sorry, Marnie, I don't buy it. It strikes me as ludicrous as pledging a college fraternity. People do ridiculous things because of an overwhelming need to be part of a club. Like your little group is the outdoorsy jock type."

"And your little group, Dawson?" Marnie shot back.

"Being a filmmaker is, by definition, a solo pursuit."

"Oh, so there's no teamwork involved?" Marnie asked. "No camaraderie between the director and cinematographer and the actors, nobody else who touches your film between the time it comes out of the factory and when we see the images up on the screen?"

"Well yes, of course—"

"So, what you mean is, we all choose which club we want to belong to," Marnie said simply. "Because everyone wants to belong."

Dawson thought about that for a moment.

"You are quite the enigma," he finally said.

"Am I?"

Dawson nodded. "There's much more to you than the jockette that meets the eye."

"I could have told you that from the beginning, Dawson. But I usually find that the guys in the drama club and the kids who work on the literary magazine make assumptions about me no matter what."

"And of course, you would never make assumptions about them," Dawson said dryly.

Marnie laughed, and for the first time, Dawson noticed that she had dimples.

Very girly-looking dimples.

"Busted," she admitted. "I have three older sisters and an older brother. My sister Kimber is supposed to be the artistic one. Jacqueline is the brilliant one. And I'm . . ."

"The jock," Dawson filled in.

She nodded.

Something made Dawson lean forward and gently push some loose hair off Marnie's face.

She looked at him, a question in her eyes.

"I vote for détente on all stereotypes," he told her.

"No more drama boys who play rugby? What a loss!" She stuck out her lower lip with playful regret.

"I'm not in the drama club," he pointed out. "But in any case, the answer is: no more jokes. Deal?"

She stuck her hand out.

He took it.

But instead of shaking her hand, he just held it. It

was like the thought he'd had at the stream—an overwhelming desire to touch her, which he'd somehow squelched.

But now, her hand was in his.

And it was clear to him that she didn't want him to let go any more than he wanted to let go.

Chapter 9

Jack wrapped the red bandana around his right hand and carefully lifted the metal coffeepot off the fire.

"You're getting pretty good at that," Darcy told him. "You won't blister your fingers today."

"Pain has a way of being a good teacher," Jack said wryly. "Coffee?"

She held out her cup, and he poured her a steaming cupful.

It was early the next morning. Jack's lean-to roommate, a guy named Stan, from Connecticut, had already left to go meet up with his own WC partner, who was camping at a site a few hundred yards away.

Darcy had come over to join Jack a few minutes later. And by the time she'd arrived, Jack had already put breakfast on the fire—fried eggs, bacon, and pancakes.

"Don't forget, a couple of tablespoons of cold water on top of that boiled coffee will settle the grounds," Jack told her. "Otherwise, you'll have brown flecks in your teeth. Not attractive."

Darcy smiled. "You really are a quick study, aren't you?"

Jack shrugged, put down the coffeepot, and turned his attention to the fry pan. This wasn't like when he and Jen used to make breakfast in Grams's kitchen—there was no automatic coffeemaker that had been set the night before, no Teflon-lined fry pans, no automatic toaster, no gas burner you could turn down if the phone rang.

Here, there was so much to pay attention to. Screw up, get distracted for a moment, and your next meal could turn into a fried mess.

"So, what do you usually have for breakfast?" Darcy asked, sipping her coffee.

"You mean in Capeside?"

Darcy nodded. "Do you have one of those moms that cooks you a hot breakfast before she lets you out the door?"

Not hardly, Jack thought. *My mother spends most of her time in a mental institution, and it's her they don't let out the door. Whether she eats breakfast or no breakfast.*

But there was no reason to tell Darcy all that.

"Actually, I live with my dad and sister, Andie."

"Oh, that pretty blond girl who's partners with that guy Peace?" Darcy interrupted.

Jack nodded. "Anyway, we usually eat cereal, toast, something like that. And coffee."

"Me too. I can't even think about real food before noon," Darcy said. "But out here, I'm starving in the morning. How'd you sleep last night?"

"Like a rock."

Jack slipped his spatula under one of the pancakes and gave it a neat flip. And then, the other one. He smiled to himself. Funny, that he'd slept so well. He'd expected to get no sleep at all for the week of playing Scout Boy. He would never have figured himself for the Joe-camper-sleep-on-the-ground type.

And yet, he'd slept better than he'd slept in ages.

"Me, too," Darcy said. She handed Jack her coffee so that he could take a quick gulp. "At home, sometimes I toss and turn forever."

"Sounds familiar," Jack agreed. "Too much on my mind, too much of the time."

Darcy nodded thoughtfully. "At night, all your problems seem bigger, don't they? Mine do. More insurmountable, anyway. Sometimes I make myself crazy, with this loop of anxiety running through my mind."

Jack cocked his head at her thoughtfully. "And here I thought you were the disgustingly well-adjusted type."

"It's an act," Darcy admitted, staring into her coffee cup. "Sometimes I think maybe everyone's acting. Most of the time, anyway."

Well, I sure as hell am, Jack thought.

"It's interesting," Jack mused, "how all the stuff I obsess about when I'm back in Capeside seems so utterly irrelevant out here."

Darcy nodded. "I broke up with my boyfriend a

few months ago. "It was . . . really hard. All our friends took sides, you know? And most of them seemed to take his side. I couldn't sleep, couldn't eat, felt like some kind of piranha at school." She laughed self-consciously. "Okay, now you think I'm really weird, right?"

Jack laughed. "Darcy, compared to my life, yours sounds refreshingly normal."

She eyed him curiously.

"Let's just say it occurs to me that everyone's life is a soap opera," Jack said. "Mine included."

"The eggs look ready," Darcy commented. "Smells great. Maybe what we both need is to spend more time making breakfast in the woods and less time obsessing about our lives, huh?" She held out her metal plate, and Jack lifted a pancake, two eggs, and three pieces of bacon into it.

"Maybe so," Jack agreed thoughtfully. He'd spent so many sleepless nights in Capeside, tossing and turning and ruminating about the minutiae of his life and his family.

It all seemed monumentally insignificant, now.

As opposed to the breakfast he'd just cooked, which was concrete, real, and crucial for them to get through the rest of the day.

He took a bite of one of the eggs he'd fried, directly from the fry pan. No sense dirtying another dish. He'd just have to wash it out.

"Good?" Darcy asked.

"Better than that," Jack told her. In fact, he'd thought he'd never tasted anything so good in his life.

* * *

Dawson knelt down on the foam pad that he'd placed on the I-dock—a long, white, pontoon dock that jutted from the WC waterfront shoreline out into Lake Perreault—and grasped the canoe paddle. To his left, on the other side of the I-dock, Pacey assumed the same position.

Pacey rolled his eyes. "I ask you, Dawson, is there anything in this world as futile as stroking with a canoe paddle on a dock that can't move? It's like taking pictures with no film in your camera."

"Frankly, I think I'd rather be paddling here than out there," Dawson said, jutting his chin in the vague direction of the water.

Not that he had any choice about it. While at WC, he knew that his life was not his own. If the Great Santori wanted all the JGs to practice paddling on an immovable dock, or to run naked through the woods while they sang "Singin' in the Rain," that's exactly what they'd be doing.

But it was amazing to Dawson how routine physical exertion could become. This morning, they'd begun the day, even before breakfast, with a three-mile run. And he'd completed it without complaint. In fact, hardly anyone had complained.

Now, every JG was on the I-dock for canoe paddling practice. Then, every JG was going to get some actual time in a canoe. And then, as the senior guides had told them, buses would be coming to WC after lunch to take the entire camp—senior guides and junior guides—to a stretch of the nearby Perreault River called "Pain Rips," where the kids would get a true white-water canoeing experience.

"Hey, Dawson," Jen called back to him, "it's the *Deliverance* moment you've been waiting for." She was fifteen feet in front of him on the I-dock, while Felicia and Marnie were side by side between Dawson and her.

"Deliverance?" Felicia piped up. "Awesome movie."

"What makes me think you watch it and root for the bad guys?" Pacey asked.

"Oh, Pacey," Felicia singsonged, "this would probably be a good time to be extremely nice to me. Or I'll have to by-mistake-on-purpose drown your ass in the Perreault this afternoon."

"The scary thing is, I believe she'd do it," Pacey told Dawson, his voice low. "There's something faintly Kathy Bates circa *Misery* about her, don't you think? Or maybe she was one of the *guys* in *Deliverance*."

"Come on, don't rag on her," Marnie said lightly. "She's pretty amazing, in her own way."

"As a means of showing your appreciation, Marnie, for the amazing girl who is Felicia, what say we secretly trade partners for the rolling-rapids experience?" Pacey asked.

"Oh no you don't," Dawson said quickly. "Marnie's mine."

Marnie flushed happily. But then she bit her lower lip. "Um Dawson, about the rapids—"

"Don't tell me," Dawson teased her. "You insist on paddling us through solo so that you earn your well-deserved place in WC heaven."

"Doubtful, Dawson," Marnie said, not turning around. "The thing is—"

The Great Santori, who was standing at the far end of the dock, holding his bullhorn in one hand and a canoe paddle in the other, cut Marnie off.

"Listen up, JGs!" he called. "We're talking stroke practice. Remember, think, and then do. Begin with the bowman's stroke, think and then do. Follow me. Do what I do."

Dawson and the others watched as the Great Santori demonstrated the bowman's stroke, so named because it was the stroke used by the person in the bow of the canoe. Then, they put their paddles in the water and imitated him as senior guides walked up and back, checking their progress.

"Now, the J-stroke," the Great Santori instructed. "Who knows it?"

Several hands went up, including Marnie's.

"Suck-up," Dawson murmured to her.

She flashed him a look he couldn't quite figure out. But before he could ask her about it, a senior guide had asked Marnie to stand and demonstrate the J-stroke, which she did.

Then the Great Santori taught the group a long series of other strokes—draws, push-aways, sweeps, and bowman's rudders.

Dawson took it all in, but his mind was only half on it. He was thinking about last night, being with Marnie, her eyes dancing in the firelight.

I wanted to kiss her, Dawson thought, *but it didn't seem like the right time or place. Still, it seemed to me as if she might have wanted me to, and—*

"All right JGs, do 'em as I call 'em," the Great Santori called.

He began to yell out the name of one stroke after another, in random order, and Dawson found himself hopelessly confused. He took his paddle out of the water.

"What's the problem, Leery?" senior guide Roger asked.

"Uh, that was a little fast," Dawson explained.

"So you think he should slow down, that it?"

"Frankly, yes," Dawson replied.

Roger nodded thoughtfully. "So, what if you're in the middle of Pain Rips and your sternman—or woman—calls out 'right rudder' because she sees rocks ahead, and you forget what to do? Think you can ask her to slow down?"

"I see your point." Dawson looked ahead to Marnie. She was executing all the strokes flawlessly.

"I'll get it down," Dawson promised.

If for no other reason than that I do not want to look like a wuss. Not this afternoon, and not in front of Marnie. No way.

Chapter 10

Jen looked down from the suspension bridge that hung fifty feet above the raging waters of the Perreault River and blanched.

It was a cauldron down there. Teeming, rock-filled, and dangerous, the Perreault River dropped several feet over the course of a half mile or so, spilling and boiling over rocks and through chutes. The roar was deafening, the white water thoroughly ominous.

Joey edged up to her. "We're going to canoe through that?" she asked.

Jen cupped a hand to one ear. She hadn't heard a word Joey said because of the din from the river.

"I can't hear you!" she yelled, exaggerating every syllable.

"We're going to canoe through that?" Joey shouted. "I can think of better ways to die!"

Jen gulped hard and nodded.

"And Elliot is going to be my partner!" Joey looked toward heaven, in hopes that there might be some divine intercession.

The only intervention came from Elliot himself, who was standing next to Joey. He looked down and turned green.

"No way," he pronounced.

"You don't have a choice about it, Elliot," Joey yelled at him.

"I'd rather stay alive, thank you," Elliot yelled back. "I gotta tell Mr. Santori." He took off to look for the SG.

"Great," Joey groaned. "I'd make out a will, but I don't own anything."

It was the middle of the afternoon, and the buses, as scheduled, had deposited all the students and instructors from Wilderness Camp at a suspension bridge over the Perreault River. Then, the canoe-carrying trucks had brought the canoes to the top of the rips and unloaded them, before coming back down to a spot below the bridge, where—theoretically at least—the JGs were going to take their canoes out of the water after negotiating the set of rapids.

Teams of JGs were being sent, two at a time, to the top of the rips. So far, Jen, Joey, and their partners hadn't been summoned. Yet.

Chav came up next to Jen. He looked down without comment.

"You up for this?" Jen asked him.

"Sure," Chav replied.

"You know, it's okay to admit you're not macho man in every single situation," Jen told him.

He gave her a cool look. "I'll try to keep that in mind."

Jen made a face. "Has anyone ever mentioned how impossible you are?"

Chav laughed. "Oh, yeah."

"Hey, do you know who's going first?" Joey shouted to Jen.

"I heard Roger say Dawson and Marnie!" Jen yelled back. "They're in the first canoe."

"Poor Dawson," Joey said. "I bet he wishes he was anywhere but here."

At the top of the rips, a half mile or so away, Dawson and Marnie were, as Jen and Joey thought, in the first canoe scheduled to run the rapids. Dawson was in the bow of the vessel, his life jacket securely fastened around his neck and chest, a bicycle helmet on his head, so that if the canoe capsized, he wouldn't dent his skull on the rocks. Marnie, the more experienced canoeist of the two of them, was in the stern.

In the center of their canoe knelt Roger, the senior instructor. But he wasn't going to do anything more than ride along, he'd made it clear. Yes, he had a paddle. But it was stowed carefully below the thwarts of the canoe, to be used only in the event of a dire emergency.

"Just take it right out into the slow water way above the top of the rips," Roger instructed. "We'll get our bearings. You've walked the rips and picked a route through?"

"Done that, will do," Dawson said. He had expected to be petrified of this, but strangely, the idea of running these rapids wasn't scaring him at all. In fact, it seemed exciting, even exhilarating.

Maybe Marnie's personality is rubbing off on me, he thought, grinning to himself.

"Hey, a little less levity and a little more attention," Roger advised. "Dawson, you're the first person to see rocks and chutes, so once we get into the soup, keep talking. If you don't say what you see, Marnie in the back won't know what to do. Got it?"

"Got it," Dawson assured him.

"And remember, there are only two ways to control your canoe in white water. Paddle faster than the water, or go slower. I suggest you go faster, there's less chance of getting rolled. If you do get rolled, get away from the canoe. Don't worry about it. It's Fiberglas; it won't die. Okay?"

Dawson nodded his agreement. "Marnie, you ready?" he called over his shoulder.

Silence from the back of the canoe.

"Marnie?" Dawson asked again, turning around.

Marnie sat there with her paddle flat across the gunwales of the vessel. "I can't, Dawson," she said, her voice shaking. "I can't do this."

At first, Dawson thought it was a joke. He expected Marnie to break into a big smile, and then he'd hear her sweet laughter ringing over the cacophony of the churning water.

"Marnie?"

"I . . . I c-can't," she said. Her face was frozen, her knuckles white.

It was then that Dawson realized she was serious. He shot Roger a quick look, but Roger was studiously examining his cuticles. Clearly, he was leaving this in the hands of the kids.

"You can do it, Marnie," Dawson encouraged her. "It's just water."

"I can't," Marnie repeated, her voice quavering even more. "It's like I can't even lift my arms. I thought maybe this time I could tough it through, that the rapids wouldn't be so terrifying but . . . oh, God, I'm so scared, Dawson."

Tears pooled in her huge, frightened eyes.

What is she referring to? Something bad that happened to her in the past? There's no time to find out now, Dawson thought. *I just have to talk her through this.*

Dawson looked over at Roger again, to see if he was going to intervene.

He wasn't.

That was when Dawson's stomach took a high dive, complete with double somersault.

I can't let her know how badly she's freaking me out, Dawson realized. *She has to believe that I have faith in her.*

Dawson shot Marnie a reassuring grin over his shoulder.

"Marnie, you're such a great canoeist. I saw what you did down on the dock," Dawson said encouragingly.

"No rapids," Marnie managed. "No movement. No canoe. That was easy."

"They won't put us into a situation where there's any real danger."

"How do you know that?" Marnie retorted, her voice rising. "People die in rapids all the time! It happens so fast, there's no time to help, no matter how hard you try. Dawson, I can't do this."

"Marnie, it's going to be okay."

Dawson jerked his head back around, toward the bow of the canoe. He had noticed something. The current of the Perreault River was carrying them right to the top of the rapids. The pounding, rushing water was merely fifty yards away, now.

Roger sat stock-still, and Dawson figured that he knew exactly what was going on. Dawson and Marnie were going to be in the rapids in a matter of seconds, whether they wanted to be or not.

Dawson gulped. There was no way that he would be able to control the canoe without Marnie's help. They were a team. Without her, it would be a disaster. They really would capsize.

"Marnie," Dawson said, his head swiveling between the top of the rips and his partner in the back. "I understand that you're scared. I understand that you're petrified. But we're going to be in the middle of those rapids in a moment whether you want to be or not. And I know you can do this."

"No," she whimpered.

"We're not out here," he told her, his voice firm and steady. "We're still on the dock, practicing. Do you hear me, Marnie?"

"We're . . ."

"Say it!" Dawson yelled. "We're still on the dock . . ."

"P-practicing," Marnie said.

"Right. And you have it completely under control."

The pounding of the river was louder, the canoe picking up speed. Dawson saw Roger tighten his hands on the paddle underneath the gunwale, which meant that the instructor would intervene if he had to. But so far he was waiting.

Clearly, something from Marnie's past was creating the terror in her now. Dawson could sense that.

"Whatever happened before isn't happening now!" Dawson yelled. "You can do it, you can."

And then, they were in.

"Paddle!" Dawson screamed.

If she doesn't, we may die.

The canoe shot forward into the roaring cauldron of water. "Rock left!" he called out, as water boiled over a huge boulder that threatened to eat their canoe for lunch. Instantly, almost instinctively, he thrust his pole into position for a right rudder, which turned the front of the canoe to the right.

And then he felt, rather than saw, Marnie's strong strokes, as the canoe rocketed ahead.

It was a watery inferno, with spray from the rapids as dense as thick smoke. The canoe slipped over a ledge and through a series of standing haystacks, Dawson calling out positions, Marnie yelling back with instructions.

They were approaching the suspension bridge.

"Go, Dawson!!! Woo-woo-woo!" Kids were yelling and screaming and cheering from the bridge, as Dawson made sweep strokes on the right and Marnie ruddered on the left; their canoe made a hard left turn to avoid a series of rocks and then shot forward again.

And then they were through. The current slowed, the river widened. The take-out position was just ahead, over to the left.

Five minutes later, they were stepping out of their canoe onto dry land.

"Good job," Roger told them. Then he immediately started jogging back up to the top of the rapids so he could take the ride through the rapids with another two-person canoe.

Dawson and Marnie were left alone on the riverbank.

Marnie had her head in her hands. Her long braid swept over her right cheek.

"You okay?" Dawson asked.

She nodded but wouldn't look up.

He put his hand gently on her back and rubbed in small circles. He could hear her crying.

"Do you want to talk about it?"

She sniffed, then wiped her face with the edge of her T-shirt. "I'm so sorry, Dawson." She lifted her red-rimmed eyes to him. "I almost got you killed."

"Marnie, you did great," he protested. "Whatever it is that had you so scared, you overcame it. When we got into the rips, you did everything right."

"I did?"

Dawson nodded.

"When I was just a kid, my family went on a white-water rafting trip with my friend's family," Marnie said, her voice low. "We'd all shot rapids lots of times, but these were ones we'd never been down before. Lisa, my friend, was in the canoe in front of me. Something went wrong—it happened so fast.

The canoe turned over. I heard her screaming, and her parents. They were being carried downriver, and there was nothing we could do."

Dawson put his arm around Marnie and held on tight.

"Her mom managed to grab a branch sticking out from the riverbank. But Lisa's dad and Lisa . . ."

She didn't need to say anything else for Dawson to know what had happened.

"I haven't run rapids since." Marnie gulped hard. "I thought that if I could just face up to my fear . . ."

"And you did," Dawson told her.

"But I was so irresponsible." Tears began to streak down her cheeks. "I had no right to put you in that kind of danger, just because I needed to test myself. You must hate me."

Hardly.

Gently, Dawson turned her chin to him. Then he brought his lips to hers.

It was a kiss that told him exactly how he felt about her. And "hate" had nothing to do with it.

Chapter 11

"Sometimes I feel, like a motherless child.
Sometimes I feel like a motherless child,
so far, far, far, far from home."

By the crackling light of the bonfire, Andie watched Peace's face as he strummed his guitar and sang the old spiritual.

Funny how I never realized he's handsome, Andie thought as Peace began the next verse. *I guess it's because I was so busy being annoyed by him.*

It was late that evening, and the entire Wilderness Camp was gathered around a huge bonfire. It was a WC tradition, called the Bonfire of Renewal, and as the Great Santori had explained, it happened on the night after everyone ran the rapids on the Perreault River.

"Your first real test was the rapids," he'd told them. "Many of you were scared to death. Some of you were sure you couldn't do it. You had to depend on your brains, your training, and on your partner."

And we did it, Andie thought. *I did it. Even Peace over there did it.*

Amazing.

As Peace continued singing, she looked across the bonfire at her brother. He was sitting with Darcy, Jen, and Chav. Andie couldn't remember the last time she'd seen him look so relaxed and happy.

There's no tension in his face, she thought. She felt a pang somewhere near her heart, because it made her realize how long it had been since she'd seen Jack looking like that.

Since before Capeside.

Before Mom got sick.

Before our brother got killed.

It was a long, long time ago.

"Hey, you okay?" Joey asked, nudging Andie's arm. "You look kind of lost."

"Oh, sure." Andie brushed the tears out of her eyes. "Must just be a cinder from the fire."

Everyone joined in gustily on the last verse of Peace's song, Andie included. And she clapped the loudest for Peace when the song finished.

Then the Great Santori stood up. Every eye was on him.

"And now, JGs, it's time to find out why this bonfire is called the Bonfire of Renewal," he told them.

"Please don't tell us you're going to make us walk on hot coals," Pacey begged.

Everyone laughed, even the Great One himself.

"Only metaphorically, Mr. Witter," he said, smiling. "We are, all of us, held captive by our own weaknesses, fears, pride, guilt, bad habits. And before you ask, Mr. Witter, yes—even me."

The group gave an appreciative chuckle.

"The Bonfire of Renewal is the time for you to face up to something about yourself that you want to leave behind here at Wilderness Camp. Some personal trait, some addictive behavior, some significant bad habit that you are ready and willing to give up. You make the commitment in here—" he pointed to his head, "and in here," he pointed to his heart.

"Miss Carol will pass out paper and pencils," he went on, his eyes scanning the solemn eyes of the group. "You will write down your commitment on the paper. Then fold it up, and put it some place on your person. For the rest of your time here at Wilderness Camp, every time you change clothes, everywhere you go, you will take that folded piece of paper with you. I don't care where you have to put it to make sure you have it, but you'd better have it."

He didn't bother to tell them what they'd have to do if he asked to see it and they'd lost it.

No one wanted to know.

"You all know that you have one more major experience here at WC. We won't talk about it tonight—there'll be time to go into it in great detail tomorrow. I have no doubt some of you are very worried about it."

"Two days alone in the woods?" Andie whispered to Joey. "More like petrified."

Joey nodded, then put a finger to her lips. She wanted to hear the rest of what the Great Santori was saying.

"After that experience," the Great Santori continued, "you each can decide if you have proved to yourself that you are strong enough to give up that which you wrote down. It's up to you."

"And then what?" Elliot piped up, intrigued in spite of himself.

"And then . . . you find out what," the Great Santori said, flashing his perfect teeth. "You'll know when the time is right for you to know."

A hush came over the campfire as everyone digested what the Great One had just told them.

"Don't write down the first thing that comes to you," the Great Santori instructed, as Miss Carol and three other senior guides passed out papers and pens to the junior guides. "Usually, the first choice is the easy choice.

"But life is not about easy choices. I want you to take the next hour to think before you write anything down. Think about your life, the kind of person you are, and the kind of person you want to be. Don't give yourself an easy out. I don't care what you need to do to focus. Talk to each other, walk around the compound, go for a naked swim in the lake—I don't care. It's up to you."

The Great Santori was finished. He signaled to Peace, who started to strum his guitar again:

> "To everything, there is a season
> And a time for every purpose under heaven . . ."

Miss Carol handed Andie pen and paper. Andie bit her lower lip, thinking hard about what she wanted to write as her renewal. And then the answer came to her. Even if it was the first thing she'd thought of, she knew it was right. There was no need for her to think further. And she began to write.

On the other side of the circle around the bonfire, another senior guide gave Jen and Chav their pens and paper. Jen nudged Chav, who was staring intently into the bonfire.

"I don't think you're allowed to say that what you want to give up is your partner," she teased. "You'll be rid of me soon enough, anyway."

He shifted his eyes over to her. "I haven't been particularly nice to you."

"I'd have to agree with that."

He nodded slowly. "The thing is, I really didn't want to come here."

"Hey, that's news," Jen said sarcastically. "Guess what? Neither did I."

"You don't understand. My brother's parole hearing was today. I knew they'd turn him down again, but I wanted to be there for him. Instead, I'm stuck here."

Jen tapped her pen thoughtfully against her knee. "You still haven't told me what you did to get sent here—other than ruling out major felonies, that is."

For a long moment, Chav didn't say anything. Then he turned his head just slightly, barely looking at her. "You want to go for a walk?"

Jen nodded.

Chav sprang up gracefully and reached out his hand for Jen's. She took it. And as they walked away from the bonfire, Chav had still not let go.

"Maybe you already left your bad trait behind," Dawson told Marnie. Even as others had gotten up from their places by the bonfire, to take the Great Santori's advice and wander for awhile before they wrote down their commitment pledges, neither Dawson nor Marnie had moved. "You faced the rapids. You admitted your fear and you overcame it."

Marnie smiled enigmatically. "There are a whole lot more where that came from."

"Gee, here I thought I was the only one who had multiple fears," Dawson joked.

Marnie's eyes searched his. "How did you get so nice, Dawson Leery?"

"Must have been all those years in drama club," he joked.

She laughed. "I was kind of obnoxious to you that first day, wasn't I?" she acknowledged.

"In a word, yes," Dawson agreed. "But to be fair, I had written you off as a girl-jock, which in the Big Book of Generalities meant that you lacked depth and sensitivity in equal measure."

"So, we're both guilty of prejudging each other?" Marnie asked.

"Looks that way."

"Who would have imagined," she murmured, "that I'd end up kissing the guy I prejudged."

"And who would have imagined he'd like it so much," Dawson added. He turned his head toward hers, her gaze met his. Then, his lips brushed softly against hers.

"What are you afraid of, Dawson?"

He thought a minute as he watched a stick of kindling wood jump in the fire. "Failing," he finally said.

"Failing, how?"

"As far back as I can remember, I've wanted to make movies," he told her. "Not just good movies, but great ones. Steven Spielberg, Orson Welles—great movies. And my fear . . . my fear is attaining mediocrity," he admitted. "What if I try my hardest, and it turns out that I simply don't have greatness in me?"

"The Salieri of film," Marnie mused.

Dawson's jaw fell open. Salieri was a composer who had been a contemporary of Mozart's. He had been talented and well appreciated. But he lacked Mozart's genius, and he knew it.

And that fact drove him mad.

"How do you know about Salieri?" Dawson asked Marnie. "Wait, I know. You saw the movie *Amadeus*."

"Watch it, Dawson," she teased. "You're doing it again, and it was a play first, for your information. Just because I intend to major in phys ed in college—"

"—doesn't mean you don't have a functional brain," Dawson finished. "Got it."

"And now that I've seen how well you can handle a canoe in white water," Marnie added, "I'd say you've proven your jock stripes as well."

"The funny thing, Marnie," he told her, "is how much I loved shooting the rapids. It shocked the hell out of me, to tell you the truth. But the adrenaline rush of doing it, of knowing I could do it, of meeting that challenge . . . it was nothing short of awesome."

She smiled at him. "I know."

Dawson slipped his arm around her, and she leaned her head against his shoulder.

"So what are you going to write down?" Dawson asked her.

"Beats me," Marnie told him.

She snuggled closer to him, and together they watched the leaping flames, perfectly at peace.

Jen shined her flashlight ahead as she walked down the dark path to the waterfront hand in hand with Chav.

He hadn't spoken a word since they'd left the bonfire. She was curious about him, she had to admit. And wildly attracted to him, too, in a visceral kind of way.

But maybe that was just his air of mystery.

Or how great he fills out a T-shirt, Jen added in her mind.

And then, out of nowhere, he spoke. "You were right about what you said to me before."

"And which particular piece of brilliance would that be?" Jen asked.

He chuckled. "You said I walk around with a chip on my shoulder."

"Ah, that one."

"My own mother tells me all the time I take myself too seriously."

Jen grinned. "I think I like your mother."

As she mentioned his mother, Jen could see Chav's face get stony.

"You would like her. She's an amazing woman. She gave birth to ten children and picked grapes until she got arthritis so badly in her fingers that she could barely open and close her hands."

They walked in silence for a few minutes, until they reached the waterfront. There, they sat down on the sand. The moon was high in the sky, and quite bright. There was a slight night breeze, and the moonlight reflected on the chop of Lake Perreault looked like millions of shattered diamonds.

"Beautiful, huh?" Jen asked.

"Yeah."

"You know, about your mother, there are all kinds of medicines for arthritis now," Jen said. "My grandmother—I call her Grams—was having trouble and now she—"

"There are medicines if you can afford them," Chav interrupted bitterly.

"What about Medicare?"

He was quiet for a few moments. "Jen, every day in America, thousands of people choose between eating and getting their medications because they can't afford both. Children go to bed hungry. People have no place to live. It happens all the time. That's the filthy underbelly of the land of the free and the home of the brave. It's the side people like you never see."

Jen turned to him. "Okay, Chav. You're right. I don't see it every day. And thank God I don't live it. But you're young and smart. You can stay in school, go to college, do anything you want to with your life. Because that happens every day in America, too."

Stalemate.

They stared at each other in the moonlight.

"How I got here—that's what you wanted to know," Chav said slowly. "I was walking to the bus stop to meet my mother—we can't afford a car. I saw her get off the bus. Her hands were full of groceries, and she was slow. Some boy was getting off the bus after her. He pushed into her, and she fell over. He cursed at her and left her there on the sidewalk, like garbage."

Jen's stomach turned over. "I'm so sorry."

"Don't be," Chav said. "I put my fist through his face. I enjoyed it. Then I left him there on the sidewalk like the garbage he is."

Jen leaned her back against a tree and folded her arms. "So, did you get arrested?"

"He was smart enough not to press charges."

"Why, because he's afraid of you?"

"I never bothered to ask," Chav said, "because I don't care."

"So how did you get sent here, then?" Jen wondered.

After a beat of silence, Chav said, "My mother."

Jen wasn't sure she understood. "Sorry?"

"My mother signed me up," Chav explained sheepishly. "She said I had to learn not to settle things with my fists. Believe me, you don't say no to my mother."

Jen couldn't help it—she laughed. "Now I *know* I like your mother."

The corners of Chav's mouth curled up. "Yeah. Me, too."

Jen put the sole of one running shoe up against the

tree. "You can't settle everything with your fists," she began slowly. "But honestly, if I'd been in your situation and I saw some kid do that to someone I loved, I would have put my fist through his face, too."

"Yeah?" Chav whispered.

"Yeah."

He was standing so close to her, she could smell mint on his breath, and something else delicious that was uniquely him.

"I wonder if WC partners are allowed to fraternize on a personal basis," he mused, his voice low and sexy.

"To tell you the truth, Chav," Jen replied, "I'm not a big rule follower. So, frankly, I don't care."

"Aren't we supposed to be down here thinking about our pledges?" Chav asked.

Jen answered by reaching up and wrapping her arms around his neck.

His arms snaked around her waist.

His kisses were everything she had imagined.

And more.

Chapter 12

Splash! Splash! Splash!

"Woo-woo! Woo-woo!"

As each junior guide came to the end of the three-mile, pre-breakfast run, they stripped off their shoes, shorts, and T-shirts—right down to the bathing suits they'd worn underneath. Then, they discarded their clothing on the beach, ran out onto the I-dock, and took a flying leap into the chilly water, letting out the wild whoop that had become the trademark yell of Wilderness Camp.

"Hey, Leery, eat my dust!" Jack called as he ran for the I-dock.

"No chance!" Dawson laughed, right on Jack's heels. They hit the end of the dock and took a huge jump into the water.

"Woo-woo!" they both screamed in midair.

Dawson gasped as the cold water hit his overheated flesh. It felt horrible and wonderful, both at the same time. He turned to float on his back, staring up at the early morning sun and the fleecy clouds moving across the sky.

That was when he realized . . .

I'm happy, he thought in amazement. I'm in the place I least wanted to be for spring break, doing the thing I least wanted to do, and I'm happy.

Huh.

"Water," Roger said, holding up a glassful. "Eighty percent of your body. Eighty percent of the earth. Coincidence? I think not. Water, JGs, is your friend."

It was two hours later, and the entire Wilderness Camp was once again gathered in a circle, in the same area where the bonfire had taken place the night before.

Dawson patted his shorts' back pocket. His commitment pledge was in there, safe and sound. He'd even put it inside a double plastic bag, in case he fell into a stream or sat on a muddy place or . . .

In the woods, you have to think of everything in advance, Dawson told himself. *Everything.*

Think, then do.

"Mr. Leery?" Roger asked suddenly.

"Yes?"

"Would you like to show us all the correct way to consume a glass of water in the woods?"

Dawson scratched his chin, as obviously a question like this from Roger was not what it seemed to be. Also, it was more a commandment than a request. Then he got up and walked slowly toward Roger, feeling the eyes of the rest of the JGs on him.

There's some trick to this, Dawson realized as he thought back frantically on all the things that all the senior guides had taught them over the past few days. They'd covered every possible subject having to do with life in the wilderness, and a few that Dawson hadn't even known existed.

But a correct way to consume a glass of water in the woods, other than in the usual fashion? I'm stumped.

Dawson reached Roger, who held the glass out to him. Dawson took it and raised it to his lips.

"Stop!" Roger commanded before Dawson had taken even a sip.

And of course, Dawson stopped.

"Where did that water come from, Leery?" Roger snapped.

"From you," Dawson replied. He knew it wasn't what Roger wanted to hear, even though it was the literal truth.

"Try again," Roger suggested wryly.

Dawson had no idea, so he took the most logical stab at it. "From the pump, presumably, where we've been getting our drinking—"

Roger cut him off with an annoyed wave of the hand.

"Anyone? Can anyone tell me with absolute certainty where that glass of water that Dawson was about to drown his sorrows in came from?"

A titter ran through the group, but no one's hand went into the air.

"Ah," Roger smiled. "No one knows with absolute certainty. Which is why you must remember this when you are in the woods: unless you know with absolute certainty where drinking water is coming from, don't drink it without treating it. I repeat. Do not drink it."

Elliot could not resist raising one finger laconically into the air. "Query. We're in the woods, Roger. It's not like there's lots of pollution or anything."

"Interesting theory," Roger said. "So, what would you call a twelve-point buck that died of a bacteriological infection two hundred feet upstream from where you're drawing your drinking water, and which has been putrefying in said water for the past two weeks?"

"Uh . . ." Elliot stammered.

" 'Uh' can get you killed, Elliot," Roger told him. "And the water I just described to you is the water Dawson was just about to drink."

Dawson instinctively dropped the glass. Because it was plastic, it didn't shatter.

"Good one, Leery. Beats dying of amoebic dysentery. Have a seat."

Jana raised her hand. "What about water from the lake?"

"The rule is, unless your mother handed it to you out of an Evian bottle, you treat it," Roger said.

"But we eat fish from the lake," Felicia protested.

Peace gave her a smug look. "Maybe *you* do."

Jen leaned toward him. "Better watch it or Chav will cut off your chocolate supply." It was a not-too-well-kept secret that vegan Peace had been kept in chocolate by Chav's secret stash.

Roger pretended not to hear that exchange. "What does the cooking process do to fish?" Roger asked the group.

"Kills the bacteria," Marnie said.

Roger nodded. "Exactly. This is not the place to develop a taste for sushi."

Dawson edged his way back to his place between Marnie and Jen, as Roger launched into an intense lecture on backwoods water purification and safety. Marnie leaned into Dawson in the subtlest of ways. But it made him feel warm all over.

Roger ran through a number of methods for purifying water from unknown sources, including the use of small chlorine tablets, iodine, potassium permanganate, and portable water filters.

"You've got iodine and chlorine in your packs," Roger went on. "They both work, but they both make water taste like a swimming pool or worse," Roger explained. "That's why I recommend boiling for ten minutes. And I mean, really boiling. Then, when you're done, let the water cool, and then mix it from one container to another, over and over, to bring some air back into it."

"What if there's gunk in it?" Andie asked.

"Gunk?" Roger repeated.

Andie blushed, but she nodded. "You know, dirt, mud, stuff like that."

Roger grinned. "Watch."

He took off one of his socks and then took a bandana handkerchief from his back pocket. He put the bandana inside the sock, as a liner. Then, he hung his sock from a tripod of three sticks that he had lashed together. And finally, he poured a gallon of dirty water into the sock.

It emerged clean and spilled into another container.

"Don't forget to purify it after you filter it," Roger added. "Filtered poison is still poison."

Everyone applauded spontaneously. Except Andie. She raised her hand again.

"Uh, just one thing," she said meekly. "It has to filter through a used sock?"

Roger laughed. "If you're thirsty enough, I promise you the dirty-sock thing won't deter you a bit. And remember, getting dehydrated in the woods is a really bad idea."

"Bad idea, got it," Andie nodded.

"Think, then do," Roger reminded them. "I'm just making use of what I've got on hand. You guys do the same. Okay, now, take ten, come back, and we'll talk about your final WC experience, which starts this afternoon. And Dawson?"

Dawson looked up. "Yes?"

"That water before was fine. I was just busting your chops."

Ten minutes later, everyone was seated in a circle around the Great Santori.

He turned to take in all of them. "Wilderness Camp," he said, "is a life-changing experience. You are not the same as when you arrived."

He let that sink in for a moment.

"Nor are we—" he motioned to the assembled senior guides to his right, "the same. We rode you hard when you arrived, because when you arrived you needed to be ridden hard. But as you adjusted, so did we. Amazing, isn't it? How quickly you can change and how much you can grow in a very short period of time."

Joey nodded her agreement, but even nodding her head hurt. She loosened the insect repellent–soaked bandana from her neck and stretched her head from side to side. The night before, she'd been so tired that she'd fallen asleep with some kind of stone stuck under the jacket she'd been using as a pillow.

Now her neck felt stiff and sore, and it didn't seem to be getting any better.

"Wilderness Camp ends with Wilderness Experience," the Great Santori told them. "Have any of you heard of the Wilderness Experience?"

Marnie's hand shot skyward. "It's when you take us into the woods and leave us there for forty-eight hours, with three matches, two fishhooks, a knife, and a roll of fishing line."

I'm dead, Andie thought. *If we do it as partners, Peace will leave me to go meditate under a tree while I get eaten by a bear or something.*

"Correct, Marnie," Mr. Santori said. "When we do Wilderness Camp full-out during the summer, the final Wilderness Experience is a solo. That means you're out there in the woods by yourself. Three matches, two fishhooks, a knife, and a roll of fishing line."

Jen shuddered. The idea of being stuck out there by herself scared the hell out of her. But she knew she could count on Chav. He had amazing instincts. And he was great in an emergency.

Unless, of course, we started making out and just kind of lost track of the whole survival thing, she added, smiling to herself.

Felicia's huge hand waved in the air.

"Yes, Divine?" the Great Santori asked.

"So we're with our partner?" Her voice was withering, as was her look at Pacey.

"Hey, I resemble that remark," Pacey said.

"You'll be in groups of six," the Great One replied.

"What if it rains?" Elliot asked.

"If it rains, you get wet," Santori said. "That is, unless you build a decent lean-to."

Elliot gulped in response to that. Lean-tos were not his long suit.

"There will be no crying for your mama, no excuses, and I will be confiscating Mr. Martin's chocolate stash."

Chav grinned and shrugged. The man had busted him, but it was no big deal.

"What if there's an emergency?" Joey asked.

"You'll have a cell phone."

"Yes!" Elliot said, pumping his fist in the air.

"Don't use it." Mr. Santori glared at Elliot, who shrank back next to Joey.

Joey sighed and shook her head, which made her neck hurt all over again. The idea of being stuck in the woods with Elliot for forty-eight hours did not exactly delight.

Thank God we're in teams of six, she thought, *or I'd have to write out my will before Elliot and I took off for uncharted territory.*

Pacey, who was sitting twenty feet or so from Joey,

felt Felicia's eyes on him. And they were saying the same thing that Joey was thinking.

Pacey blew her a kiss. He'd be happy to loll in her huge shadow and let her get them through this. At the moment, he was thrilled that Felicia belonged to him.

Mr. Santori paced around the circle, looking closely at his young junior guides. "Originally," he said as he paced, "our intention was to put you in the woods with your partners. But we've changed our plans."

"Huh?" Pacey asked, his head jerking around.

The Great Santori nodded at Roger to take over. Roger stepped forward. "We think you've each gotten too comfortable with your partners, so we're going to shake things up a bit. Your teams for Wilderness Experience have been grouped geographically," he told them. "For example, groups of six from Hartford and groups of six from New York will be together. Also the group from Capeside. Three matches, two fishhooks, a knife, and a roll of fishing line per person. That's it."

Everyone groaned.

"Let's make that three matches for the six of you," the Great Santori decided suddenly. "Anyone want to groan at that? We can drop down to two, if you'd like."

Silence.

"Now, back to your campsites," Santori said, taking over again. "Clean up—I don't want to see any sign that any of you have ever been there, is that clear?"

All around him, heads nodded.

"You leave your garbage behind and I will not be a happy man. The senior guides will be around to bring you into the wilderness at noontime. Any final requests from the condemned?" he joked.

No hand went into the air.

"Good. One last thing." Santori's eyes scanned over the group one last time. "Good luck. Some of you are going to need it."

Roger stopped and consulted his compass. The Capeside group stopped, too.

"Where are you taking us, O Fearless Leader?" Pacey joked.

Roger ignored him. "Follow me," is all he said. And instead of following the neat trail cut into the rolling terrain, he veered off to the right. A faint path led into the woods there and disappeared into a thicket of trees.

"I have a bad feeling about this," Andie murmured to her brother as they tromped down the path.

"It'll be okay," he assured her.

But Andie could see that he'd lost that happy, relaxed look, and clearly he was just trying to make her feel better.

The next forty-five minutes were spent in a grueling hike over rough terrain. They crossed a small stream, hiked up several hardscrabble hills and down into a swale, and finally, they emerged at the edge of a small pond. In the middle of nowhere.

"We're here," Roger announced.

"I don't suppose there's a day spa just past those trees?" Pacey ventured.

Andie wished Pacey would stop joking. She was too nervous to put up with his jokes. She scanned the horizon. There was no sign of civilization anywhere. She could have been in the exact same place two centuries before; it was that remote a location.

Her eyes met Joey's. Joey looked as nervous as Andie felt, which made Andie feel even worse.

"Someone will be back to get you in forty-eight hours," Roger told them. "Remember, think, then do."

"Who has the phone?" Jen asked nervously.

Dawson raised his hand. Roger had handed it to him just before they'd left camp.

"Hope those batteries are charged," Joey muttered.

"All right," Roger said briskly. "Sleep tight, don't let the mosquitos bite, and don't you dare use your phone for anything but the most dire of emergencies, got me?"

They all nodded.

"Have a great experience," Roger added. "See ya the day after tomorrow."

Without hesitation, he turned on his heels in the direction from which they had come. Thirty seconds later, he was gone. For a few moments, they heard the clomp-clomp of his boots in the woods, and the snap of a stick as he stepped on it.

Then, silence.

And more silence. It was eerie. All six of them stood in a circle, not really sure what to do.

Joey swung her small day-pack off her back and sat on it. Mr. Santori had been absolutely true to his word. They had been given exactly three matches to share among the six of them. Those were expected to last them all forty-eight hours. Other than that, they had the clothes they had worn in—Roger had warned them to wear as many layers as possible, despite the unusually warm spring weather—their Swiss Army knives, two fishhooks apiece, and their lengths of fishing line on a spool.

She rubbed her neck. It had loosened up only a little.

"Um . . . guys?" Andie was the first one to break the quiet. "How are we supposed to purify water if we don't have iodine, don't have chlorine, and don't have anything to boil it in?"

"I was just wondering the same thing," Pacey said. He pulled off his day-pack and sat on it, too. "I don't know about you, but I don't want to get some strange North Carolina spotted water disease."

Jen looked all around, her senses on full alert. "I don't know yet. But I do know that we've only got about five daylight hours left. And a helluva lot of work to do before nightfall. If we don't get started, we're going to be miserable later."

No one moved. No one said anything.

"Get started, as in *now,*" Jen added firmly. "Dawson, you try to dig some bait and catch us some fish. Pacey and Jack, start on the lean-to. Just one. We'll all sleep together. We'll be warmer that way, and we won't need more than one fire. Andie, you—"

"Time out," Andie interrupted sharply. "Did someone appoint you general when I wasn't looking?"

"We need to get organized," Jen replied, her voice even. "And someone has to organize us."

"Fine with me," Jack said.

"Fine with you?" Andie echoed. "Jen doesn't know any more about surviving out here than any of the rest of us know. Maybe she knows less. You can't just accept someone's authority because they decide to put themselves in charge!"

"I think you're missing the point here, McPhee," Pacey said. "This is not a coup d'état. We're just six fun-loving, basically indoor types who need to get through this hellish experience as best we can."

"Fine, I agree," Andie said. She jutted her chin out. "But we should all agree on just what that entails. Shouldn't we?"

"Excuse me, but while you're bickering, the sun is getting lower in the sky," Jen pointed out. "You want to waste what's left of the daylight, or you want to get to work?"

"Might I posit a suggestion to end this ridiculous conversation?" Dawson asked.

"Posit away," Joey said. She was too tired to care much who the leader was, as long as they were good at it.

"Can we all agree that, in fact, we need a leader?" Dawson asked the group.

"What happened to democracy?" Andie asked, her voice rising. "One person, one vote?"

"Andie, you're only being like this because you're nervous," Jack pointed out.

"Being like what, reasonable? Am I the only one that doesn't think we should blindly follow Jen's orders?"

Jen stared Andie in the eye. "And what's your suggestion, exactly?"

Andie didn't say anything.

"My suggestion is we vote on a leader," Joey said. "How's that?"

"I second that," Dawson said quickly.

"It's a plan," Pacey agreed. "All righty then. By a show of hands, who thinks Jen should be our leader?"

Dawson, Jack, and Pacey's hands shot into the air.

"I'm abstaining," Jen explained. She looked over at Joey and Andie. "Well?"

Joey's hand slowly went up.

"So, what, I'm outvoted?" Andie asked.

"We were hoping this could occur by unanimous consent," Dawson said. "Unless you have an alternate suggestion?"

Andie shook her head no. And slowly, her hand went into the air, too. "I just hope you know what you're doing, Jen," she said darkly.

"I hope so, too," Jen said. "Now, let's get organized. Because if we don't get a lean-to built, and a fire going, we're gonna be in major trouble."

Chapter 13

Dawson sat alone at the end of the pond farthest from their campsite.

Across the way, he could see Jack and Pacey laboriously putting up a large lean-to. They'd cleared an area on the ground of stones, sticks, and other obstructs, and dragged in a long, downed tree, which they'd propped up in the V of another tree's split trunk. Now, they were busy propping sticks, and other material against the main support beam.

It was hard work, and every once in a while, Dawson could hear one or the other of them grunting with effort.

Jen, Joey, and Andie weren't idle, either. Jen had sent Joey on a recon mission around the pond and into the nearby woods, both to get a better sense of their surroundings and also to see if there was anything in the woods that could possibly be scavenged.

"You never know," Jen had told Joey before Joey had set out. "If people had camped here before, they might have left behind something that we could use."

"What?" Joey had asked blithely. "A cookstove, six sleeping bags, and a battery-powered TV/VCR combination with a collection of the American Film Institute's top one hundred films of the last century?"

"I'd settle for a rusty bucket that we can use to boil water, so keep your eyes open," Jen replied. "Now, please get going, and don't lose sight of the pond, no matter where you go. I don't want to organize a search party."

Andie had stared at Jen, her arms folded defensively, awaiting orders.

"Find a sharp stick, or use your hands, and dig a trench around the lean-to. If it rains, we don't need water sloshing in."

"And do you do anything besides dictate who does what?" Andie asked.

"Yes, Andie, I do," Jen said evenly. "Wood patrol. We're going to be here for forty-eight hours; we're going to need a huge woodpile. And it has to be kept under something so it won't get wet. I'll probably have to make a lean-to for the wood myself."

After Jen said what job she had reserved for herself—tough and dirty—she and Andie headed off on their respective missions.

Leaving me, Dawson thought, *to make sure we don't starve.*

Dawson unwrapped his bandana, which was on the ground. Inside it was a squirming, wriggly mass of grubs and worms, which he'd found by rolling over a huge rock near the side of the pond.

"Supposedly, we can eat these," he said aloud, as he looked at the unappetizing mess. "But somehow fish holds more appeal."

He reached into his pocket, took out one of the precious fishhooks, and tied it to the monofilament fishing line. Before he'd even started to look for bait, he'd tied one end of that line to a tree and stretched it out, to see just how much line he had to work with. About a hundred feet, he'd discovered. Not a lot, but enough.

He picked up one of the earthworms and impaled it on the fishhook. Then, he took the hook and tried to flip it into the pond.

It went exactly three feet.

"Idiot," he said to himself. "You need weight, or it won't go anywhere."

He looked around for a rock that he might tie onto the line to use as a weight, and saw a long, thin one that might be perfect. Quickly, he wrapped a couple of loops around the stone—it couldn't have weighed more than an ounce or so—and tied it off. It hung there perfectly.

I hope this works, he thought as he drew back the rock-and-hook combination. Then he flung it toward the pond.

It went five feet before slapping weakly into the water.

"Nothing's going to bite there," Dawson lamented

aloud. He sat down anyway and tried to think. How could he get the line to go out further into the lake? His musing was interrupted by a WC-trademark war whoop.

"Woo-woo! Bingo!"

A few second later, Joey came tearing out the woods about fifty yards to the north of Dawson, with something in her hand.

"What'd you find?" Dawson called to her.

"Gold!" Joey yelled back. She jogged over toward Dawson. "Actually, better than gold at this stage in our late adolescence. Gold wouldn't do us any good. However, an empty Coke can is incredibly useful. Whoever littered in the woods, don't tell the Great Santori that I said thank you."

Dawson grinned. Joey was right. With an empty can, they'd have something in which to boil water. Which meant they'd be able to drink. Of course, unless they found a way to save their boiled water, they'd all be drinking hot H_20 in shifts for the next two days, but at least they wouldn't die of thirst."Good job, Joey," Dawson said to her. "That's a real—"

He stopped.

"What's wrong, Dawson?" Joey asked. "Because—"

But Dawson was lost in thought, looking at Joey's Coke can. Then he looked at the fishing line left at his feet after he'd managed to cast all of five feet into the pond.

And a lightbulb went off his head. It was such a good idea that he laughed aloud.

"Give me that," he told Joey.

"Have you lost your mind, Dawson?" Joey responded. "That dirty can is the most important thing we've got, at this point."

"Exactly," Dawson told her. He pulled the fishing line from the water, and Joey reluctantly handed him the can.

Joey gave him a dark look. "Consider yourself warned, Dawson. Lose that and you're going to be sleeping with the fishes."

Dawson didn't reply. Instead, he started to do what he'd seen in his mind's eye. First, he tied one end of the fishing line in a loop around the can, and tightened it securely so it couldn't possibly come loose. Then, he wound the rest of the line in concentric circles around the can, tight enough so it would stay, loose enough so that it could come free if he wanted it to.

"Dawson, what are you doing?"

"Thinking, then doing," Dawson told her. "Watch."

He unhooked the waterlogged, nearly dead worm from the hook that now dangled a foot below the Coke can and impaled a new one. Then he let out a little more line so that he had about three feet to work with, at the end of which were the stone and the hook-impaled worm.

"Wish me luck," he told Joey, who was still regarding him very skeptically. He held the Coke can in his left hand and took the end of the fishing line in his right hand. Then, he swung the line around and around in a circle perpendicular to the ground until it had gained a lot of speed.

And, finally, he let it fly.

It shot out toward the middle of the pond, and the line flew off the Coke can as easily as if it were an expensive fishing reel.

Joey laughed out loud. "The term brilliant springs to the lips," she told him. "I had no idea there was a nature boy hiding in there. You may need to reconsider film school."

"Thanks," Dawson said modestly. "But it won't do us any good unless—"

WHAM! There was a huge pull at the line as a fish in the pond immediately struck at the worm, felt the prick of the hook in its mouth, and shot for the surface of the pond.

A silvery green fish exploded toward the sky, walked on its tail for a foot or so across the surface, and then dived back into the water.

"Don't lose it, Dawson!" Joey exclaimed.

Dawson had no intention of losing the fish. But his heart was pounding hard—as hard as it had the first time he'd kissed Joey in tenth grade. He was so afraid he'd make a mistake, break the precious fishing line, lose one of their precious fishing hooks, lose their precious dinner.

All of his concentration was on the squirming thing at the end of his makeshift fishing pole. He played the fish very carefully. Ten minutes later, a four-pound largemouth bass was on the bank next to him and Joey.

"I love you!" Joey whooped, throwing her arms around him and hugging him hard.

It was reflex. His arms snaked around her neck in response.

Neither moved. They were eye to eye. Their lips were a mere inch apart.

"Uh . . ." Joey finally mumbled. "This was supposed to be about catching us dinner. Wasn't it?"

"At the moment, I appear to have forgotten," Dawson replied.

As if by mutual agreement, they finally stepped away from one another.

"We can pretend that never happened," Joey said nervously. "Too much fresh air has us both in an altered state of consciousness."

"If you say so," Dawson replied, because at the moment, he felt as if he could have just stood there, holding Joey, forever.

He forced himself to focus on fishing. One fish was good, six would be better. He dispatched the bass with his knife, cleaned it quickly, and had another worm back in the water within ten minutes.

Joey and he were all business. As if their intense hug–almost kiss had never happened.

Pacey walked back to the campsite, holding his jacket in front of him.

"What've you got?" Jen asked him, pushing around the coals of the fire she'd built.

He opened up his jacket. "Water chestnuts," he said. "Dozens of them. We can roast them. Also, I found a blackberry bramble, but they won't be ripe for another few months. Bummer."

"Fish and water chestnuts it'll be," Jen told him.

"For breakfast, lunch, and dinner, for the next two days," Joey added, coming up behind them.

"Hey, in certain trendy New York restaurants you pay top dollar for this sort of thing," Jen pointed out.

"Zee specials zis evening are fresh feesh," Dawson said, doing his best French accent. "We have ze sunfish, catfish, or bass, and madame can choose broiled, broiled, or zer house specialty, broiled."

"When can we eat?" Joey asked. "My stomach is making a serious racket."

"How about now?" Jen suggested. "Incidentally, there're about two gallons of purified water in that sinkhole over there. I boiled it while you guys were working. I lined the hole with my waterproof jacket. Seems to be holding," Jen explained.

"Jen, you're a marvel of backwoods ability," Jack told her. "Who would have guessed?"

"Certainly not me," Jen admitted. "I figure we've got another half hour of daylight. Let's eat and clean up so we don't attract flies."

The water chestnuts went directly on the coals of the fire, and everyone took fillets from the fish Dawson had caught, impaled them on green sticks that wouldn't burn, and held them over the hot coals of the fire. The fish fillets sizzled as they cooked.

"Mmm," Pacey said, taking a bite directly from the end of his stick. "Half-cooked, half-charred catfish. It's so *Deliverance,* isn't it?"

"More like the setup for a slasher movie," Jack said.

"Oh, thank you," Joey moaned sarcastically. "Now I'm sure I'll sleep like a baby."

For the next few minutes, no one said anything. They were too busy devouring the fish. And then, the water chestnuts were ready. It was an unusual dessert, yes. But under the circumstances, it was more tasty than any of them could imagine.

By the time they were done eating, it was deep twilight.

"I wish that was only an appetizer," Joey said sighing.

"Well it isn't, so let's not dwell on half-empty stomachs," Andie said. "Now what?"

"We could sit around the campfire and tell ghost stories," Pacey proposed.

"I definitely pass," Joey pronounced.

"I was thinking sleep," Jen suggested. "Tomorrow, we can improve this campsite, maybe set a deadfall for some animals, do some more fishing. We can't do any of that at night. Sleeping will conserve our energy."

"Who said 'Early to bed, early to rise, makes a man healthy, wealthy, and wise'?" Pacey asked. "Was it Thomas Jefferson? Principal Green? Courtney Love? Or Benjamin Franklin?"

"Duh, Pacey. Benjamin Franklin," Andie replied.

Pacey eyed her solemnly. "Is that your final answer?"

She laughed. "Yes, Regis. Do I win the million?"

"Well, I, for one, am ready to pack it in," Joey said, rubbing her neck.

"Still bothering you?" Dawson asked her.

"Kind of. It seems ridiculous that a little thing like that should bother me out here in the middle of nowhere."

"Listen, you guys," Jen began, "we'll need to keep

watch on that fire overnight. Jack, why don't you take the first shift? Come in and wake me in, say, two hours."

Jack nodded his assent, and Jen started toward the lean-to. The others looked at each other, not sure what to do next. They weren't exactly tired, but there didn't seem much point in staying awake, either. So they followed Jen to the lean-to.

"Who wants to call room service?" Pacey quipped. "A few porn tapes on the tube, pop a few brewskis . . ."

"Too much cable TV rotted out what little brain you formerly possessed," Joey told him.

Dawson folded his arms. "It's going to be really cold tonight unless we use body heat. My suggestion is we sleep together, spoon-style."

"All of us?" Joey asked.

"Unless someone has a better proposition for conserving body heat."

Silence.

"Dawson's right," Jen finally said. She lay down on her side and looked up at her friends. "Well?"

Pacey lay down in front of her on his side. She put her arm around him.

Soon they were five sardines in a tight row—Jen, Pacey, Andie, Dawson, Joey.

"Jack, in a couple of hours, wake the person on the end for them to take their turn guarding the fire," Jen called. "That would be me."

"You got it," Jack called back.

"Only one question," Andie asked from the middle of the pack. "What if one of us has to pee?"

As soon as she said that, they all felt the urge to go. Which they all fought off.

Dawson could smell the sweet, familiar scent of Joey's hair. He slowly pushed it off her neck. "Still hurt?" he whispered.

She nodded yes.

His hands began gently to knead the muscles in her neck. He could feel her relaxing under his fingers. Touching her felt like the most natural thing in the world.

Dawson fell asleep with the scent of Joey's hair in his nose and his warm hands on her neck.

Fifteen minutes later, all five of them were snoring.

"Good morning, Mr. Witter."

Pacey looked up blearily. And blinked. He was on predawn fire watch, and he hadn't slept very well. So maybe he was hallucinating.

"I must be dreaming," Pacey said evenly to the visitor. "I am suffering from sleep deprivation and you are but a figment of my imagination."

"You're not dreaming; you're on Wilderness Experience at Wilderness Camp," the familiar voice said to him. "And I must say, you've got quite the little campsite here."

Pacey rubbed his eyes again. But he wasn't dreaming. Principal Green stood in the middle of their campsite clad in jeans and a flack jacket

"So, Principal Green, what brings you to our little home away from home?" Pacey asked. "Keep your voice down, sir, I don't want to wake my comrades in crime. Or should I have them join the welcoming committee?"

Mr. Green smiled and squatted down beside Pacey.

"There's no need," he said, his voice low.

Pacey looked over at his principal and scratched his chin. "I must say, it is a surprise to see you here."

"I told you that I might drop in on you and your friends," Principal Green reminded Pacey.

"That you did, sir. You must have been hiking in the dark to get here."

"Not really. I'm camped about a half mile from here. I come here on many of my vacations. It's a wonderful part of the country, really."

Pacey laughed. "So, if we had gotten into any serious trouble . . ."

"I was not more than a holler away," Mr. Green filled in. "But my money was on the six of you."

Pacey let that information sink in for a moment. "I wish I could offer you some coffee or something, but of course, we haven't got any. How about some delicious piping-hot water?"

The principal smiled again. "I have to tell you, Mr. Witter, that I'm very, very impressed with the way you and your cohorts are performing. That's quite a fire, quite a woodpile, quite a lean-to—altogether an impressive campsite."

"You said that before," Pacey told him. "If you'd like to help us build a deadfall later, we can use all the help we can get."

"I have a feeling you'll do just fine, son."

Their silence was comfortable as Pacey watched the sun begin to peek over the horizon.

"Funny," he finally told the principal. "I haven't found this experience quite as odious as I had anticipated."

"And why do you think that is, Mr. Witter?"

Pacey thought a moment. "I know you'd like me to say that I found this character-building, sir, but frankly, that's not it."

"What, then?"

Pacey shrugged. "Somehow, leaving Capeside feels like leaving all the baggage of Capeside, if only for a little while. When you're busy figuring out how to survive, it's tough to obsess about the usual minutiae of life."

"Son, that's what I would call character-building."

"Yeah?" Pacey smiled ruefully. "Well, I'm hoping this can be our little secret. It would ruin my rep."

The principal held his hands out to the fire. "I know you think I sent you out here as some sort of punishment, but nothing could be further from the truth. I wanted all six of you to see the potential I see in you. And that potential is not limited to million-dollar words, or pseudo-intellectual jingos, or pithy comments about life, love, and the art of celluloid."

"You've noticed all that about us, eh?" Pacey asked wryly.

"And more. But that's a start. You've accorded yourself with flying colors, Mr. Witter. I'm proud of you."

Pacey was surprised how much that touched him.

Maybe because I've so rarely heard anything remotely like it from my own father.

"Thank you, sir." Pacey said. No joke followed. No ironic quip. He just left it at "thank you."

Principal Green stood up and stretched. "Well, I believe I'll finish my early-morning constitutional."

"Hold on." Pacey stood up, too. "If you leave now, when I tell the rest of them you were here, none of them will believe me."

"Good point." Principal Green reached into his pocket and pulled out a business card, which he handed to Pacey. "There's your proof."

He stuck out his hand to shake Pacey's. "You're going to go far in the world, Mr. Witter. Of that I am certain. And I'm an excellent judge of character."

Pacey could actually feel tears come to his eyes. He was glad the principal had turned away, because he didn't want to have to explain them.

A while later, when the whole gang had awakened, Pacey told them Principal Green had made a dawn visit to their campsite.

"Oh, ye of little faith." Pacey pulled Mr. Green's business card from his pocket. "I offer into evidence exhibit A."

"That's A as in: Are you kidding, right?" Joey asked. "What does a business card prove?"

"It's just like you to make this up, Pacey," Dawson agreed, "and plant that business card in your pants."

"Thank you for that vote of confidence in my imagination," Pacey said, "but it just so happens I'm telling the truth."

No one believed him. And soon everyone was too

busy doing work that might possibly lead to a breakfast other than grubs and worms to even give it any more thought.

Pacey just put the business card back in his pocket, right next to the piece of paper on which he'd written his commitment pledge.

Soon he'd be throwing one into the fire. But the other he planned to hold onto for a long, long time.

Chapter 14

"I look around me, and I see fifty young people whose minds, bodies, hearts, and spirits have grown immensely during the past week," The Great Santori said.

The circle of JGs surrounded the final bonfire of the week. In the distance, they thought they could hear the idling diesel engines of the buses that were waiting to take them back home.

Dawson's eyes scanned his fellow JGs, now all clad in their Wilderness Camp Junior Guide T-shirts. They'd earned those shirts. When Miss Carol and some other senior guides had passed them out this morning, they'd all felt proud to put them on.

Next to him, Marnie smiled sadly. "I can't believe it's almost over," she whispered.

"Neither can I," he whispered back.

"Think of who you were and how you were just one short week ago," Mr. Santori continued. "Some of you were trying to work the angles, sure you could figure out a way to get out of here."

His gaze fell on a chagrined Elliot.

"Others of you figured you could buy your way out. Or be mean enough to shut everyone here out. Or make enough jokes to prevent you from getting in touch with anything real."

Some self-conscious laughter rippled through the group.

"Funny how you're all still here," Mr. Santori said. "The truth is, you could have walked away. This isn't a prison and you all knew that. And when we left you in the woods for forty-eight hours without chemicals to purify water, you had your cell phones. No water constitutes an emergency. Only none of you used those phones."

Smiles of pride spread from face to face. It was true. No one had used their cell phones. Not even Elliot.

"What you didn't know was that there were adults camped within a half mile of each of you," Roger said, taking over for The Great One. "You were always safe, we were always looking out for you. But the awesome thing is, none of you needed us. You proved that you could look out for each other, and for yourselves. You did it."

The proud smiles broke into ear-to-ear grins.

"Soon you'll be going home," Roger broke in. "But the you who returns home will never again be the you who came here a week ago. Miss Carol?"

"That's right," Miss Carol agreed. "Notice how I haven't even had to yell at you guys, or blow my whistle, in the past seventy-two hours? Once you took responsibility and grew up, I started treating you with grown-up respect."

The Great Santori took over again. "And now, JGs, comes the most solemn moment of your Wilderness Camp experience. Before your team test in the woods, you all wrote down a character flaw, bad habit, fear, or addiction that you desire to leave behind when you leave here today. You've had those slips of paper on your person all this time. Would you all please put them in your hand now.

"This moment is between you and your soul," Mr. Santori told them solemnly. "Read your pledge. Look deep inside yourself. If you feel you've earned the right to let go of it, and if you're truly ready to accept that challenge, then feed your commitment pledge to the fire."

The circle was hushed, the only sounds the birds flying overhead and a slight wind rustling through the trees.

"There are no points for doing it, you don't win anything, and no one will ask what your pledge was, or if you threw it into the fire." Mr. Santori looked around the circle again. "It's between you and you. And it's all up to you. Maybe now you realize, it always was. And it always will be.

"The entire staff will leave you alone for the next hour," Mr. Santori said. "There are no rules. You can talk, walk, be silent, cry, laugh, whatever feels right to you. And if you're man or woman enough to feed your commitment pledge to the fire, you'll know that, too."

With a curt nod, the Senior Guides all followed Mr. Santori down the path to the waterfront at a healthy jog.

Around the circle, low conversations broke out. Some kids got up, to stand alone. Some lay down and stared up at the blue sky. Others formed little groups and talked.

Marnie's hand slid into Dawson's. The two of them just sat there in a silence that felt sacred, staring into the fire.

Peace found Andie, and sat down next to her. "I wanted to tell you that you turned out to be an excellent partner."

Andie grinned. "And you aren't quite the stoner I had you pegged for."

"Different strokes for different folks, right?"

"Right," Andie agreed. She looked down at her commitment pledge: stop being so judgmental, it read. With a last smile at Peace, she got up and threw her pledge into the fire.

On the other side of the circle, Jen stood up and stretched. Then she began walking away from the fire. She looked back at Chav, raising her eyebrows as in, what-are-you-waiting-for?

An invitation, evidently. He was by her side in an instant, and they headed into the woods.

Pacey sought out Felicia. "Felicia, Felicia, Felicia," he said.

"Brady Bunch II?" Felicia asked. "The first movie stunk up the theater, so don't go thinking sequel."

"I was thinking more along the lines of how much I admire you, actually," Pacey said.

Felicia snorted back a laugh. "Yuh."

"You're a strong woman, and you're proud of it. That's admirable."

Felicia gave him a dubious look. "Pacey, I really hope it says 'quit being such a suck-up' on that piece of paper."

"Not at all—"

"Look, Pacey, let's cut to the chase. I know guys like you. You feel threatened by a girl as large and strong as I am. Like somehow I can't possibly be sexual, or even thought of as feminine, because of my size."

Pacey reddened. He didn't speak. Because he knew she was speaking the truth.

"Well, here's a news flash for you. A girl who power lifts can want love and romance just as much as some bimbo who shakes her headlights on *The Man Show*. She can be just as feminine. And a whole hell of a lot more a real woman than those caricatures."

She opened her pledge and read it to him: stop denying that you have a feminine side because you're afraid of being rejected.

She fed her paper into the fire.

Pacey watched it burn. "So, I'm pretty much a butt-hole, right?"

"Past tense, I hope," Felicia said. She held out a meaty palm.

Pacey shook it. "You're quite a woman, Felicia."

"Thank you, Pacey. I think you might be on your way to being quite a man."

Pacey chuckled and unfolded his pledge. Stop fulfilling your lowest expectations of yourself.

"Ready?" Felicia asked him.

"More than." He, too, fed his pledge to the fire.

"Excuse me," Joey interrupted them. "Have you seen Elliot?"

"I heard Chav impaled him on a stick of green wood and weinie-roasted him," Pacey said.

Felicia gave him a dark look, but then she burst out laughing.

Joey wandered away from the fire, but she didn't see Elliot anywhere. She did, however, almost stumble over something in the brush.

Two somethings.

Chav and Jen. Seriously intertwined.

"Oops. Sorry. Really sorry." Red-faced, Joey backed away. For a moment, she was shocked. Then she realized that if she and Dawson had been alone when he was massaging her neck . . . well, who knows what might have happened?

Maybe that's why wild is part of wilderness, she thought wryly.

"Joey!" Elliot was hurrying over to her. "I've been looking for you everywhere."

"I've been looking for you, too."

"I just want to say that you were a really good sport about being my partner," Elliot told her. "I'm not exactly Mr. Nature."

"Hey, you didn't use the phone," Joey reminded him. "You shot the rapids. You did everything everyone else did."

"Under duress," Elliot admitted. "I know The

Great Santori wants us to have a power moment, here, but trust me, nature and I coexist much better with a computer and a four-star hotel between us."

"Well, at least you know yourself, Elliot," Joey pointed out.

"That I do. Uh . . . I was wondering if I might hug you."

"Yes, Elliot. You might."

He wrapped his skinny arms around her. For a moment, her chin rested on top of his shoulder, then he released her.

"Well, I don't know about you," Elliot said, "but I've been wanting to do that since the day I met you." He held out his hand and opened his fist. His commitment pledge lay there in a wad.

"Read it," he told Joey.

She uncrumpled the paper. *Stop being such a wuss with girls,* she read. She handed it back to him. "You're on your way, Elliot."

"Care to share yours?"

"Not really," Joey told him. "I gotta go."

She took off. She needed some time by herself, to decide whether or not she was ready to feed her pledge to the flames.

On the other side of the fire, Jack stood with Darcy.

"Ready to throw yours?" he asked her.

"I already did it," she replied, "while you were lost in thought."

Jack nodded pensively. Then he stuck his pledge back into his pocket.

"Not ready?" she asked him.

"Not yet. Soon. Maybe." With a smile, he walked away.

Jen pulled her lips away from Chav's for a moment and looked into his dark, piercing eyes. "Thinking about your pledge?"

"Too busy thinking about you." He pushed some hair off her forehead, and kissed her temple.

"Going to think about your pledge?"

He hesitated, then shook his head no. "The whole think is a little too easy for my taste. I don't need some guy with great bridge work and a big fire to make a ritual out of my life."

Jen grinned at him. "We seem to have much more in common than either of us gave us credit for."

"Maybe so. So, you ever get to Philly, Jen?"

She held him even closer. "Read my lips."

And he did.

Elsewhere in the woods, Dawson walked a path, hand-in-hand with Marnie.

"I don't want this to end," she told him.

He turned to her. "I never expected to say that I share some of those feelings, but I do."

Her eyes searched his. "Will we ever see each other again, Dawson?"

"I hope so, Marnie."

"You were right, you know. I did face my biggest fear on the rapids. Thanks to you."

"Thanks to yourself," Dawson told her.

Her arms snaked around his neck. "I'll never forget you, Dawson Leery."

"And I'll never forget you."

His mouth came down on hers in a sweet, heartfelt kiss.

Neither of them heard Joey as she headed down the path. She hadn't been looking for them, or for anyone, but she'd found them just the same.

And it was stupid, really, that she got such a terrible pang near her heart, watching Dawson kissing Marnie. They were very far from being a couple anymore. She had no reason to expect that he wouldn't be kissing other girls, to have such a horrible reaction just because some other girl was in his arms.

But she did.

Quickly, she turned around to flee.

But not before Dawson saw her. "Joey," he called.

She just pretended she hadn't heard him, and kept on running.

"Bye!"

"Bye, I had the greatest time!"

"Write to me, you guys!"

As the JGs climbed onto their buses, heartfelt goodbyes rang through the air.

Dawson and Joey were the last two to get on their bus. Joey took the very back seat. Dawson sat next to her. The bus rumbled to life. Joey stared out the window.

"You okay?" Dawson asked her.

"Sure."

The bus passed under the arches, then hit the country road that would take them to the main road, then the freeway, and then back to a life far, far away from Wilderness Camp.

"So, Marnie and I got to be close," Dawson told her awkwardly.

"So I witnessed."

"She—"

"You hardly owe me any explanations, Dawson," Joey told him, cutting him off.

That's true, Dawson thought. *I don't. So why do I feel like I do?*

"All in all, that was a pretty amazing experience," Joey finally said.

"Maybe Principal Green's brighter than we gave him credit for," Dawson said.

Joey nodded. Finally, she turned to him. "Listen, you don't have to answer this if you don't want to, Dawson. But did you throw your pledge into the fire?"

He moved the big toe of his right foot against his pledge, which was inside his sock. "No. Did you?"

She felt the corner of her pledge dig into her underneath her belt. "No." She hesitated. "Mine was about you, Dawson."

"Funny," he said. "Mine was about you."

They shared a special smile that only the two of them could understand, and they headed for home.

About the Author

C. J. Anders is a pseudonym for a well-known couple who write young-adult fiction.

Dawson's Creek™

Trouble in Paradise

An ALL-NEW, ORIGINAL STORY Featuring the characters of Dawson's Creek

Here comes trouble...

To promote fall tourism, Capeside has a new slogan, "Fall in Love in Capeside," and a new weekend romance festival, including a kissing marathon. Pacey can't wait, but Andie's not interested. Then there's the contest for best romantic video that Dawson's dying to win, if only he could decide who should get the female lead.

Jen's visiting cousin Courtney might be just right for the role. She's not acting mean anymore. She's actually...nice. *Way* too nice, think Joey and Jen. And their instincts are right, because when Courtney starts scheming, watch out Capeside!

Based on the hit television show produced by Columbia TriStar Television

Published by Pocket Books

2075-01